The Sleepover Club

Three fantastic Sleepover Club
stories in one!

Have you been invited to all these sleepovers?

Mega
Sleepover Club ⑤

Sleepover on Friday 13th
Sleepover Girls go Camping
Sleepover Girls go Detective

Louis Catt
Fiona Cummings

Collins

An imprint of HarperCollinsPublishers

The Sleepover Club ® is a registered trademark of HarperCollins*Publishers* Ltd

Sleepover on Friday 13th first published in Great Britain by Collins 1998
Sleepover Girls Go Camping first published as *Sleepover Girls at Camp*
in Great Britain by Collins 1999
Sleepover Girls Go Detective first published in Great Britain by Collins 1999

First published in this three-in-one edition by Collins 2002

Collins is an imprint of HarperCollins*Publishers* Ltd
77-85 Fulham Palace Road, Hammersmith
London W6 8JB

The HarperCollins website address is www.**fire**and**water**.com

3 5 7 9 10 8 6 4 2

Sleepover on Friday 13th
Sleepover Girls Go Detective
Text copyright © Louis Catt 1998, 1999

Sleepover Girls Go Camping
Text copyright © Fiona Cummings 1999

Original series characters, plotlines and settings © Rose Impey 1997

ISBN 0 00 712843-6

The authors assert the moral right to be identified as the authors of the work.

Printed and bound in England by
Clays Ltd, St Ives plc

Sleepover Kit List

1. Sleeping bag
2. Pillow
3. Pyjamas or a nightdress
4. Slippers
5. Toothbrush, toothpaste, soap etc
6. Towel
7. Teddy
8. A creepy story
9. Food for a midnight feast:
   chocolate, crisps, sweets, biscuits.
   In fact anything you like to eat.
10. Torch
11. Hairbrush
12. Hair things like a bobble or hairband,
    if you need them
13. Clean knickers and socks
14. Change of clothes for the next day
15. Sleepover diary and membership card

Sleepover on Friday 13th

by Louis Catt

An imprint of HarperCollinsPublishers

CHAPTER ONE

It's odd, isn't it? I mean, Thursday the 7th, or Monday the 24th – I bet you never even notice those days! Well, not unless it's your birthday or something like that. I mean, have you ever forgotten your own birthday? No! Of course not – and I'd never forget mine – it's June 9th, the best ever time of year to have a birthday because it's exactly half way between Christmas.

And I'd never forget the birthdays of the rest of the Sleepover Club either. Not that they'd let me! Just imagine if I forgot Frankie's birthday! She's my best mate, but she'd still kill me if I forgot. Actually, I suppose I'd kill *her* if she forgot *my* birthday – but I bet we'd make up soon after. Frankie and I are like that – we're always arguing, but it doesn't mean anything. Frankie says we argue because I'm a Gemini and I can't ever make up my mind (which isn't true). I say it's because she's an Aries and she's a pig-headed ram. Well, maybe she isn't exactly pig-headed – but she does like to boss us about…

Lyndz has four brothers so it always seems to be someone's birthday in her house. Her mum makes just the coolest birthday cakes! She used to be a domestic science teacher, and she's a whizz at cooking. When Lyndz's little brother, Ben, was four her mum made him a chocolate cake in the shape of a gorilla, and it was the scrummiest thing you've ever eaten. Lyndz's birthday is in October. Frankie says she's a typical Libran – easy going and always trying to keep the peace. She even seems to like her brothers.

I don't know how I'd feel about four brothers. Lyndz says it's OK, so maybe it is. I've got two older sisters, Emma and Molly. And believe you me, two sisters is the worst thing that could ever happen to anybody, especially when one of them is like my sister Molly.

Nobody has got a sister as awful as she is – I call her Molly the Monster, and I think that's being really nice. The worst thing is we have to share a bedroom, and she fusses and moans non-stop. I can't leave one sock on her side without her going *mad*. And what's really unfair is she won't even let me keep my rat in the room! I tell her it's cruelty to animals, but she doesn't listen. She just puts on this stupid face and says, "Oh Laura, I do wish you'd grow up!" She knows I hate it when anyone calls me that. The rest of the Sleepover Club call me Kenny, because of my surname – McKenzie.

Fliss has her birthday soon after the summer holidays and she starts planning her cake the second term starts… not to mention all her presents! One year she had a cake covered with little pink roses and purple ribbons. Frankie said she just *knew* Fliss would be wearing purple ribbons in her hair – and she was! All the presents from Fliss's mum were tied up with pink and purple string – and you can guess what colour the balloons were! Fliss's mum must have spent ages and ages getting everything to match... but she's like that. I think Fliss is, too. Maybe it's because she's a Virgo. Frankie says Virgos like everything to be perfect.

Rosie's the fifth member of the Sleepover Club. Her birthday's July 15th. The last one after mine. Rosie's mum makes a huge thing about her birthday. I think it's because she worries that Rosie doesn't get as much attention as her brother and sister, so she makes it up to her then. Frankie and I were talking about it the other day, and we both think Rosie deserves a special birthday.

But hang on, I'm sidetracking. Why was I talking about birthdays? Oh yes! I was saying that mostly people don't notice what day and date it is... but Friday 13th. *Eeeeeek*! You always notice *that* date. And that's the day we had this *totally* scary sleepover at my house. I'll tell you all about it in just a minute... it was brilliant.

I don't know if you're superstitious. I'm not, not really – but Friday 13th *does* make you feel a bit creepy, doesn't it? And if you drop a cup, or fall over, or break something, you can't help thinking it all happened because it's an unlucky day, even if you fall over twice as much on other days.

It's also a great day for telling horror stories and, as you know, I *love* horror stories. I know some true ones, too, because my dad's a doctor, and sometimes he tells us stories about what happened in the old days. Did you know that doctors used to saw off people's legs while they were still wide awake? It's true. They'd give them a bit of leather to chew on, but that's all. And when they were finished they just threw the old leg into a bucket – and by the end of the day the bucket was full of legs!

Does that give you chills up and down your spine? It did when Dad told me – but I'm going to be a doctor when I grow up, so I've got to get used to all that kind of stuff. I practise by watching TV programmes like *Casualty* – and even when there's blood everywhere, I love it!

I told the Sleepover Club about the bucket full of legs and Frankie said it was the best story she'd heard in ages. Fliss said it was disgusting – she's a bit squeamish about things like that – but she still went and told her younger brother. And then her mum told me off because he woke up in the night screaming.

I think it might have been the leg story that started Frankie and me thinking about Friday 13th. Frankie had the idea to have a sleepover on that night, but it was my idea to make it a really really special one... well, I'm sure you'll agree, it was much too good an opportunity to miss. We were going to make sure we had the creepiest, scariest

Sleepover on Friday 13th

Friday 13th ever!

Lyndz and Rosie thought it was a brilliant idea. Only Fliss didn't, which wasn't a great surprise. She said she couldn't come because she goes to tea with her dad and his new baby on Fridays.

Frankie stared at her. "But you're always home by about half-past six," she said.

Fliss wriggled, and went pink. "I might have to stay later," she said.

Frankie shook her head. "Felicity Sidebotham," she said, "are you scared?"

Fliss went even pinker. "Of course I'm not," she said, but her voice was a little bit wobbly.

Lyndz patted her arm. "It'll be OK," she said. "We'll just have a lot of fun."

"Yes," Frankie said. "Lots of *scary* fun!"

"I'm not scared!" Fliss said, but she still sounded squeakier than usual.

"So does that mean you'll come?" I asked.

"Of course I will," she said. "Just as long as you don't go too far."

That made me laugh. I told Fliss she

13

sounded just like her mum. Fliss tossed her head and said she didn't, but we all knew that that was exactly what her mum would have said. Looking back on it now, maybe we should have taken more notice... but of course, we didn't!

CHAPTER TWO

Everyone came round to my house after school the next day so we could sort out a plan. A Friday 13th *super* plan! We grabbed a packet of choccy biscuits, some crisps and a coke each, and sneaked up to my room. Molly the Monster was out somewhere, so we piled up the pillows and duvets from her bed and mine and made ourselves really comfortable.

"We need to make a list," Frankie said. "Where's a pen?"

I found a stubby old pencil under my bed. It's always exciting, looking under my bed.

The weirdest things pop out sometimes, and I know I haven't put them there.

I mean, there was the time when Emma lost her best trainers. Anyone would have thought she'd lost the crown jewels, the way she went on about it. She kept looking at me, too, and she knows I don't have the same size feet as her. Well, not quite. I have to stuff loads of extra socks on if I want to wear Em's shoes.

Anyway, even Dad got involved and he ordered a *huge* search. And guess where they were? Yes – that's right. Under my bed! I told Dad they must have walked there by themselves, but he just made a sort of *humph*! noise.

The problem was, in the hunt Mum found Molly's homework diary under my bed, and Monster Features said it was *my* fault! Can you believe it? I never touched her diary, and if I'd known it was there I would've given it back to her. I don't want *anything* of Molly's in my half of the room.

Then Dad went on about the other

things... two pairs of jeans (dirty), one sweatshirt (crumpled), one bag of rat food (just a little bit open), last week's maths test (scrumpled), half a bar of chocolate (melted), lots of bits of paper, an empty coke can, one clean blue sock, one smelly green sock, one bedroom slipper, three pens, an old rubber... and some very interesting fluffy bits.

Mum had a go at me, too, and Molly moaned and groaned. It went on for ages. Personally I don't know what they were fussing about.

But there I go, sidetracking again. I was telling you about our sleepover, wasn't I? So, anyway, I found the pencil and tore a piece of paper out of an old notebook. Then we got planning. Frankie wrote down:

1. Check sleepover OK with Kenny's mum.
2. Get rid of Molly.

I sighed when she put down number two. Some chance! If Molly has a friend to stay I'm quite happy to make myself scarce and share Emma's room. There's always loads of interesting things to poke around in in there, so you'd think Molly would be pleased to do the same for me... but oh, no. She hates moving out of our room, and she hates all my friends, too.

"Maybe she'll be away that night," Fliss said hopefully.

I began to giggle. "Yeah – after all, it *is* Friday 13th! Maybe she'll be off scaring small children!"

"Frightening little old ladies!" said Lyndz.

Rosie sniggered. "Turning the milk sour on people's doorsteps!"

"Sending murderers screaming home to their grannies!" Frankie shrieked.

That cracked us all up. We rolled about on the floor, we were laughing so much. Some coke cans fell over and the crisps got scrunched into the carpet, but we just couldn't stop.

At last we sat up, and I scrabbled around for the piece of paper. It had got very soggy, so I tore out another sheet and we started again.

"What shall we do about food!" I yelled.

We all started grinning at each other. As you know, food is a favourite Sleepover Club subject.

"Green spaghetti!" said Frankie.

"Green pizza!" said Lyndz.

"Green jelly spiders!" shrieked Rosie.

"Green jelly worms!" said Fliss with a shudder.

Frankie looked excited. "Maybe we could make a huge bowl of green slime! We could put the jelly spiders and worms in it – and then everyone has to eat them without using fingers!"

"Yeah!" I said. "Cool!"

We've only just discovered green slime. Actually, it was Lyndz who invented it. Rosie was round at her house and they were helping Lyndz's mum make green jelly. Lyndz was supposed to be stirring the jelly cubes in hot water to make them melt, but she was talking to Rosie and didn't stir them enough. Then she put in just a bit too much cold water by mistake.

"Whoops!" Lyndz said. "Oh well. I don't suppose it'll matter," and she tipped the whole lot into the bowl where it was meant to set... but it never did! It turned out all slithery and – well, slimy. The bits of jelly cube that hadn't quite melted were floating on the top. When Lyndz and Rosie fished them out and ate them they were like jelly sweets – all rubbery. Ben, Lyndz's little brother, thought it tasted gross, but Lyndz didn't, and neither did Rosie. They ate the whole lot... with straws! We've been eating green slime ever since. It's a Sleepover Club special!

"What else?" Lyndz asked. "What other food is creepy?"

I was playing with the pencil. "Um... I don't know."

"OK." Frankie snatched the pencil off me and turned to face us all. "So what sort of things shall we do? How can we set it up so it's really scary?" She wrote *Plans*! on the paper, and drew a creepy face with long pointy teeth underneath.

Fliss gave a little shiver. "We don't want to go too far…"

We all started eyeballing each other and Fliss quickly shut up.

"Booby traps!" I said. "We ought to have booby traps! And horrible noises!"

Frankie let out a loud and horrible wail. She was sitting right next to me with chocolate crumbs all over her face… but still it sent a quivery chill up my spine. Fliss squeaked, and Rosie and Lyndz clutched each other.

"Wow!" I said. "Maybe we could tape you! That'd sound completely gruesome in the dark—"

I didn't get a chance to finish. Frankie gave another wail and grabbed me. "Kenny. You're a genius! That's it. We'll make the spookiest tape ever, full of shriekings and wailings!"

"And horrible gurglings!" shouted Rosie.

"Slow dragging footsteps!" yelled Lyndz.

Even Fliss was beginning to look enthusiastic.

We were so excited we didn't hear the banging. We were all jumping up and down on my bed, and I was waving a pillow round and round – just as Molly burst through the door. It wasn't my fault she walked straight into the pillow.

"*Ooooh*!" Molly made an amazing spluttering noise and sat down on the bed with a flump. She looked so funny we all fell about laughing.

It was a pity Mum was right behind her. We had really and truly meant to tidy up all the crisps and crumbs – and of course we were going to make the beds. It's always the same though, I expect you've noticed – no one ever surprises you when your room is all neat and tidy and spotlessly clean. No, it's only ever when it's totally upside down. And upside down was exactly what my half of the room was – and Molly's half wasn't much better.

We got it sorted out. Well, we had to. Mum stood in the doorway with her arms folded until it was back to normal. Molly tried to boss us about, too, but luckily the phone went and Mum sent her downstairs to answer it and she was gone ages.

I didn't ask Mum about having a sleepover straight away. It didn't seem quite the right moment. Just then she seemed really keen on getting rid of everybody – not on having them around. Still, I wasn't too worried, I was sure I could find a way round her somehow, even if it meant doing the washing-up or some other gruesome task for a week. It was going to be the best sleepover ever – and nothing was going to stand in our way – we just had to make sure Molly didn't stick her nose in and spoil it!

CHAPTER THREE

After the gang had gone I went back inside expecting to find Molly waiting to yell and scream and throw a fit or two – all in my direction. I was ready for it – but it never happened! She was in the kitchen talking to Mum, and as I went past she actually waved at me – if you'd been there you would have heard my jaw fall *thunk* on the floor. I leant against the wall to recover. Yes, OK I leant against the wall to recover *and* to see if I could listen in and find out what was going on. Wouldn't you have done the same?

"That's fine," I heard Mum say. "It'll be

24

nice for you to have a night away with a friend, and it's not as if you have school the next day. You can collect your things when you get home from school, and I'll give you your bus fare then."

My jaw thunked on the floor for the second time in minutes. Molly going away? With a friend? And then it clicked... Mum had said she wouldn't have any school the next day – Molly was going to be away on Friday night!

It took a ginormous effort not to dash to the phone that second and ring Frankie and Fliss and Lyndz and Rosie. But somehow I restrained myself. Somehow I managed to stay where I was until Mum and Molly had finished chatting, and Molly was back on the phone.

"Zoe?" she said. "Mum says it's OK. I'll zoom home from school and get my stuff, and then I'll catch the first bus over."

As soon as Molly was out of the way I wandered into the kitchen trying to look as if I didn't really want anything. Mum was tidying up, so I thought it might be a good idea to hang up a few mugs. After all, it wasn't *that* long since I'd been blasted for being messy, untidy, and a few other things that I couldn't remember.

Mum looked at me suspiciously. "Hmm," she said. "Let me guess... you want to have a sleepover here on Friday night." Then she nodded. "I don't see why not. It'll be much easier for you with Molly away – but I want your room spotless by the time she comes back again!"

I gave her a huge hug. "I promise!" I said, and I meant it. Cross my heart and hope to die. Then I helped put away all the rest of the crockery.

I had to wait until school the next day to tell the others. Mum said the phone bill was already staggering under the weight of all my calls, and I'd only said goodbye to my friends half an hour before. When I burst into the cloakroom and told them that the sleepover was all fixed *and* Molly was going to be away Frankie whooped, Lyndz cheered and Rosie grinned all over her face. Only Fliss shuffled a bit.

"What's the matter?" I asked. "You're not chickening out after all, are you?"

Frankie banged Fliss on the back. "You said you'd come!"

Lyndz nodded. "It wouldn't be the same without you," she said.

Fliss started to look really pleased. For a moment I felt bad, and I wondered if we were a bit hard on Fliss sometimes.

Then she shuffled her feet again. "It's the burglar," she said. "My mum isn't sure if I should spend the night away from home."

We all stared at her. "Burglar?" Rosie said. "What burglar?"

"It was in *The Mercury*," Fliss said. "Three houses were broken into last week, and another one this week. One of the houses was just round the corner from where I live!"

Frankie gave a loud snort. "You'll be just as safe at Kenny's house as you are at home," she said. "After all, it's only a burglar

– it's not a murderer."

Fliss went even pinker. "My mum says it might not be safe. She says burglars often murder people if they get in their way."

Frankie made another snorting noise, but Lyndz patted Fliss's arm. "We could come and collect you," she said. "I could ask my mum to drive us both to Kenny's house."

Fliss looked a lot happier. "That would be great," she said.

I wasn't really taking much notice. *I* was thinking that things were getting better by the minute. Friday 13th – no Molly – a spooky sleepover – and now a burglar on the loose! What more could we ask for?

"Hey!" I said. "Maybe we could hunt down the burglar and catch him! Is there a reward, Fliss?"

Lyndz gave me a push. "Shut up!" she hissed, because Fliss was staring at me in her rabbit-caught-in-the-headlights kind of way. Catching burglars was about the last thing she would think of as fun.

"Just kidding," I said, but I didn't look at

Frankie. I was pretty sure that she was thinking the same as me. But we didn't have time to discuss the sleepover any more, because the bell for registration rang.

At lunchtime we got into a huddle to talk about the food, and Fliss was a lot more cheerful. She said she'd make a green cake, and when Rosie said she hoped it would be green inside, as well as having green icing, Fliss giggled and said, "Of course it will."

I wondered if Fliss would have green hair ribbons to match.

"Bags I make the green spaghetti," Rosie said. "I'll put currants in it, and they'll look like dead flies."

"Or spiders without legs!" said Fliss, and we all laughed.

Lyndz said she'd already had an idea for a scary pizza. "What?" Frankie asked, but Lyndz shook her head and wouldn't say. She's completely brilliant at cooking so we didn't make her tell us. If she had a good idea it was worth waiting for!

"I don't mind doing the green slime and the jelly spiders and worms," I said. "But what are you going to do, Frankie?"

Frankie rolled her eyes. "Wait and see!" she said. "Slugs and snails and puppy dog's tails!"

"Yuck!" said Fliss, but she didn't look totally grossed out.

You know I said how my jaw kept falling open so I looked like a gasping goldfish? Well, it happened again. As I staggered in through our front door that afternoon, I met Emma coming out with some girl I didn't know.

"Hi," I said, although I didn't expect a reply. Sometimes Emma pretends I'm invisible when she's with someone. Either that, or she talks to me as if I'm about six and she's my ageing aunt. Today I was lucky, this time it was the ageing aunt.

"Hi," she said, and ruffled my hair. She knows I hate it, but she still goes on doing it. "Look, Jade – this is my kid sister, Laura."

Jade gave me the sort of look you'd give a passing beetle. "Oh," she said.

"She's got loads of funny little friends," Emma said. "They have a club, and they all sleep over at each other's houses. Cute, isn't it?"

Jade didn't look as if she agreed, but she nodded anyway. "Yeah. Cute."

Emma ruffled my hair again. "You can really have fun on Friday, little sister," she said. "I'm going to stay with Jade for the weekend. And she and the strange girl walked off.

I stood and stared after them, my jaw doing its thunking thing. Emma was going away for the *whole weekend*. Wow! And an idea crept into my head, and once it was there it grew and grew and grew: if I put all Molly's things in Emma's room, I could clear my room right out! For the first time ever we could have loads and loads of space!

I could just imagine it. No Molly hanging around telling us not to touch her things. No squeezing three extra sleeping bags onto the tiny bit of floor between my bed and Molly's. I could push Molly's bed right against the wall, push the dressing table back… or we could move the beds the other way… I dashed to the phone to tell Frankie, and to ask her to come round as early as she could on Friday to help.

Frankie was just as pleased as I was. Then she said something that I'd been thinking. I'd been *thinking* it, but not saying it on purpose. I suppose I was being superstitious – you can't be too careful around Friday 13th, can you? But then Frankie came right out and said it.

"It all seems too good to be true," she said. "Isn't Friday 13th meant to be an unlucky day?"

So I'm blaming all the things that happened after that on Frankie.

CHAPTER FOUR

I woke up really early on Friday 13th. Molly was still fast asleep with her mouth wide open. *Gross!* I thought about seeing if I could flip something in, but I decided not to. After all, she was going to be away for the night of our sleepover. Maybe if I was nice to her she'd go away again...

I decided to start fixing up some of the booby traps and tricks ready for the evening. Frankie was coming home with me after school to make our scary tape and to help move the bedroom furniture... but I thought there was no harm in getting started. And anyway, I had to plan something special for Frankie! I slid out of bed and tiptoed out of the room.

Down in the kitchen I had a good look round. I knew exactly what I wanted to do – I wanted to arrange something so that Frankie had a fright. Yes, I know she's my very best mate – but she wouldn't be angry with me, she'd just think it was really funny. Besides, I had a sneaky feeling that she might have a plan or two up her sleeve for me, too.

I stared at the cupboards, hoping for inspiration. It didn't help much, so I opened a few doors and peered in. Flour? Could be useful. Sticky syrup? Maybe. I opened a jar of raisins, and ate some. Looking at them made me giggle – they looked just like mouse droppings! A few in the corner of my room might be fun… Fliss might be fooled for a minute or two! But what could I do that Frankie wouldn't expect? She was bound to be suspicious of drawers and cupboards in my room… I needed a much more cunning idea! I ate a few more raisins and climbed on a stool to look in the top cupboard... and then it happened.

Whoooooosh!

I nearly died of fright. Something soft and dusty and furry flew straight at me. I fell off the stool with a crash. My heart was pounding and my knees had turned to jelly as I stared wildly... at my old hot-water bottle!

OK, OK, I know. hot-water bottles are pink and rubbery. But remember when you were little and relatives gave you furry, cat-cover hot-water bottles, and brown, teddy hot-water bottles, and cosy clown hot-water bottles? One Christmas I had *four*! Talk about boring. And I hate hot-water bottles anyway – I'm always worried they might burst and splurge boiling water all over me while I'm asleep.

So Mum had put them away. And obviously this was one of them. I picked it up. It was a furry black cat, but it was totally covered in dust – it must have been in the top cupboard for ages and ages. Then, while I was looking at it, a ginormous light bulb switched itself on in my head. This was it! This could be my special surprise for Frankie! After all, it had scared *me* silly; I was still feeling fluttery inside. As it had done that to me – wouldn't it do just the same to Frankie? Yes! I said to myself. *Yes! Yes! Yes!*

I was about to put the cat back exactly how it had been, when I had another thought. I grabbed the bag of flour and gave it a thorough dusting... just for that little extra effect. Then I climbed back on the stool. I could see why the cat had sprung out the way it did. The cupboard was so small I had to bend the hot-water bottle to fit it in, which made a natural spring! I grinned happily as I wiped my hands and put the flour back on the shelf.

"Laura? Don't tell me you've got up early just to make your old dad a cup of tea!"

I jumped in a guilty sort of way, but Dad didn't notice. He was looking his usual morning self – all crumpled, and half-asleep.

I didn't want to make him suspicious, so I put the kettle on without making a fuss, while he got out the teapot and cups. Then I made us both some toast, fetched the paper and we sat down to breakfast together.

"This is a very pleasant surprise," Dad said, and he yawned. "It'll set me up for a terrible day. I've got surgery, then house calls, and then this evening I've got to go to a meeting... and I'm introducing the speaker so I've got to dash back here and get all dressed up in my suit."

"Poor old Dad," I said, and I meant it. He works really hard and is always having to dash around all over the place. It's a tough life being a doctor – but that hasn't put me off!

"Look at this!" Dad said suddenly. He was reading the paper. "There's been *another* burglary! In just the next street. Well, they'd better not try getting in here. There's nothing for them to take, but it won't hurt to be careful."

"I'll make sure all the doors and windows

are shut before I leave," I said. "And I'll tell Mum to be extra careful, too."

After I'd finished my toast I went to get ready for school. Molly looked very surprised when she saw I was up before her, but she didn't make any nasty remarks. I decided it must be because she had a friend. Wow, I thought. This is actually turning out to be a Really Good Day!

All through assembly I kept thinking of how I'd jumped when that dusty old cat flew out at me. It made me smile, and Frankie started to give me sideways looks.

"What was so funny?" she asked when we all met up at first break.

"Nothing," I said. "I was just thinking about tonight."

Lyndz gave a little whoop. "Just wait till you see my pizza!" she said. "Tom helped me – we had a totally ace idea!"

"My spaghetti's turned out a bit odd," Rosie said. "We didn't have any green food colouring so I thought I could mix blue and yellow, but it hasn't really worked."

"You should have phoned me," Fliss said. "My mum bought two kinds of green for my cake."

Frankie nudged at me. Trust Fliss.

Fliss saw the nudge, and pulled a face at us. "My mum says if a thing's worth doing, it's worth doing well. Anyway, you haven't told us what you're bringing yet, Frankie?"

"Ah! Wait and see. It's a surprise," Frankie said.

"I didn't see you carrying anything to school," Fliss said. "And aren't you going straight home with Kenny?"

"Congratulations!" Frankie banged Fliss on the back. "I proclaim you... Felicity Sidebotham, Junior Detective!"

"I was only wondering," Fliss said, sounding all huffy.

"Well, you'll just have to keep guessing," Frankie said. "Nothing will be revealed until tonight... the night of Friday 13th!" And she made a ghoulish face.

Rosie squeaked, and we all laughed – Fliss

too. Then the bell went, and we had to go back into lessons.

That afternoon, on the way back from school, I looked at Frankie's school bag slung on her back – Fliss was right, it didn't look as if there was anything much in it at all.

"Have you really made something for tonight?" I asked.

"Wait and see!" Frankie said, and I knew it wouldn't be any good asking her any more about it. She's brilliant at keeping secrets. I wouldn't find out about this one until she was ready!

CHAPTER FIVE

Emma wasn't there, of course, when Frankie and I crashed in through the front door. She was already safely on her way to her friend Jade's house. Molly was still at home, though. She growled at us when we charged into our bedroom.

"Can't you two kiddies go and play somewhere else? I'm *trying* to get my things packed!"

Honestly. You could tell Molly hadn't stayed the night with anyone for years. She had two sets of pyjamas on the bed, three pairs of socks and four different T-shirts –

she looked as if she was going away for weeks! I could have told her all she needed was a toothbrush and something to sleep in, but I didn't. I pulled Frankie out of the room and we went down to the kitchen. It looked cleaner and tidier than usual; the floor was positively gleaming! A note from Mum lay on the table:

CAKE IN TIN. DON'T MAKE A MESS –
NEW NEIGHBOUR COMING IN FOR TEA.

"Ace!" Frankie said. "I love your mum's cakes." She went to the tin and got the cake out while I found us some coke.

"We might as well eat down here," I said. "With any luck Molly will be gone soon – and then we can really get busy. I haven't made the slime jelly yet."

"OK." Frankie cut two huge slices of Mum's cake. It was chocolate – and one of her very best. The icing was thick and gooey, and the cake was soft and squidgey. Awesome!

We were cutting ourselves a second piece when the doorbell rang.

Frankie jumped up. "That might be for me!" she said, and we both raced for the door.

Frankie's mum was standing outside, and she was holding two big cardboard boxes.

Frankie let out a loud whoop and rushed towards her. "Mum! You're a star!"

"I know." Frankie's mum smiled, and handed one box to Frankie, and the other to me. "But don't think I'm going to make a habit of running round after you! Have a good time – and I'll see you tomorrow."

"Quick," Frankie said, as her mum hurried back to the car. "We've got to get these in your freezer!"

"What are they?" I asked, puzzled.

"I'll show you when we're inside," Frankie said. "But they'll have started melting on the way over, so hurry up and open the front door!"

"It *is* open—" I began, and then I saw that it wasn't. It must have swung shut while we were talking to Frankie's mum.

We looked at each other in horror for a

second, and then I remembered. "It's all right," I said. "Molly's in."

I put the box down and rang the doorbell like crazy. Nothing happened at first, so I rang even harder and started hammering on the door.

At last Molly heard me, but she didn't come to the door. She opened the window upstairs and leant out.

"Who is it?" she called, sounding very nervous. "Why are you making so much noise? My dad's here! He's very angry!"

I stood back so she could see me. "Molly! It's me! Open the door! And hurry up about it!"

I can't believe Molly sometimes. She is *so* mean. Of course any normal, decent person would have come and opened the door if they saw their sister stuck outside. But, as you know, Molly isn't a normal, decent person and she didn't – she just stared at me.

"What are you doing out there?" she asked.

"Just open the door!" I yelled.

Frankie was peering into the box she was holding, looking anxious. A trickle of something red was creeping out of the bottom.

"I'm busy," Molly said, and would you believe it? She slammed the window shut and disappeared.

I jammed my finger on the doorbell so it sounded like a fire alarm – but it didn't make any difference. My horrible ghastly monster sister just ignored it.

"Can't we get in through the back door?" Frankie asked.

We rushed round the side of the house, but the back door was firmly locked. We tried every window, and I even attempted climbing up a drainpipe – but it was useless. Our house was like a super-safe prison – and we were on the outside.

I shook my head gloomily, as we walked back round to the front. "It's no good," I said. "It's because of all the burglaries. Before Dad went out he told me and Mum to keep everything triple locked. And I know all the downstairs windows are shut because I locked them myself."

"Fantastic," said Frankie, and she sat down on the front step. I gave the doorbell one last punch. It gave a weird clunk, and stopped ringing. When I tried again, nothing happened.

"Well, that's blown it," I said, and sat on the step beside Frankie. The trickle of red from the box was longer now. It looked exactly like blood, and I stared at it.

"Frankie – what exactly is in these boxes?"

Frankie sighed heavily. "It was the best thing ever. Look!" And she opened the first box. Inside was something that looked exactly like a head with pale green sightless eyes gazing up at me. Well, it was almost like a head, but a head that was getting softer and squishier by the second.

"Wow!" I gasped. "Sculpted ice cream. It's utterly *awesome*!"

"It was," Frankie said. "I spent hours on it. The eyes are grapes, by the way… they're probably all that'll be left soon."

"What's in the other box?" I asked, and she opened the lid. Inside was a plate with a melting block of – frozen blood?

"It's beetroot and raspberries mashed up," Frankie said, and she sounded even more gloomy. "I was going to mash it some more and put the head on it… but it's ruined now."

"I'll kill Molly," I said.

"Maybe we could put *her* head on the plate," Frankie said, but at that moment it didn't sound much like a joke.

Suddenly I sat up. I'd thought of something to make us feel more cheerful. "Hey," I said, "Molly's going to be in *mega* trouble with Mum for shutting us out! It's all Molly's fault that this has happened."

"Yeah," Frankie agreed, and we both felt a tiny bit better.

We sat on the step for at least ten minutes watching Frankie's ice-cream head gradually dissolve. Actually, after two minutes we gave in and ate some of it. After all, we couldn't let it go to waste, could we? But it wasn't long before it was just a soggy mess with the two grapes swimming in the middle.

"Do you think we'd better move the other box?" Frankie asked. "It seems to have made a bit of a mess."

I looked across, and she was right. The blood mixture was dripping all the way down the steps. "Hmm," I said. "It's a pity we can't leave it like that. It'd be a great entrance for the others – blood on the doorstep!"

Frankie laughed, but we both knew my mum wouldn't agree with us. Mums are so boring when it comes to things like blood.

"Hey, Frankie!" I leapt to my feet. I'd suddenly had an amazing flash of inspiration. "We could still use it! We could make a trail of blood drops!"

Frankie's eyes shone. "Wicked! *A trail of gruesome spots leads the detectives in and out of the bushes and trees. In and out they hurried, until they found—*"

"A body!" We both yelled together, and then we collapsed, laughing.

We did a fantastic job – we made the most life-like trail of blood you ever saw. It started just round the corner of the house, because I didn't want Mum telling us to wash it away before we'd shown Rosie, Lyndz and Fliss. We started with a few drops, and then a few more – and then a big puddle. Actually, we didn't mean to make it quite so big but the plate slipped.

Frankie said it didn't matter. "We can pretend that's where the victim tried to pull the knife out of his back," she said.

It looked wonderfully ghoulish.

We put a few more drops on the bushes, but there wasn't much mixture left to do anything else.

"We ought to make a body, and half-hide it under the bushes," I said.

Frankie nodded. "Or we could just leave half a body!"

You can see why Frankie's my very best

friend. She likes blood and gore as much as I do!

After we'd finished the blood trail we took both boxes round the back of the house and dumped them in the bin. Quite a lot of the melted ice cream dribbled out on the way, but there wasn't anything we could do about it. We couldn't get back into the house to fetch any buckets of water or anything like that. If anyone said anything, it was all Molly's fault.

As we wandered back to the front door Mum came walking up the path with some strange woman beside her – our new neighbour!

"This is our house," Mum was saying. "It's—" And then she saw us. Her jaw did the thunking open thing mine's been doing for days, but the woman screamed. She really did! And she clutched at my mum!

Mum is made of steel. She put her jaw back in place, and glared at me. "Is this your idea of a Friday 13th joke?" she began. "Just *look* at the state you're both in!"

She was right. Frankie and I did look rather gruesome. I suppose the beetroot mixture had got all over us while we were laying our trail.

"Mum," I said. "Mum, it really and truly isn't our fault – we got locked out and Molly wouldn't let us back in!"

By the time we'd finished explaining what had happened, Mum was steaming mad with Molly, just as we'd hoped.

"That's it!" she said. "There's no way that young lady's going out tonight. She's grounded!"

Frankie and I gasped. That wasn't part of the plan. Mum couldn't do that – not *tonight*!

But she did. Even though I begged her not to. Even though Frankie begged her not to. We pleaded. We said it was all our fault. But it was no use. The new neighbour didn't help, either. She kept going on about how dangerous it was, us two little girlies being outside with a manic burglar tramping round the area. That made up Mum's mind. Molly was not going anywhere that night.

Frankie and I made faces at each other as we tipped soapy water over the front steps.

"If only the door hadn't shut," I said. "That was so unlucky."

Frankie nodded. "Friday 13th," she said. "Bad luck day!"

And it was only just beginning…

CHAPTER SIX

Mum realised how unfair it was that Molly being grounded had ruined our plans for the sleepover, so to make it up to us she said we could have the sleepover in Emma's room – as long as we *promised to be careful and not spoil anything*.

But thanks to Molly the Monster we were only just getting ready to make our scary noises tape when Rosie arrived. We didn't hear her, of course, because of the doorbell not working and Emma's room being at the back of the house, so Molly came and told us Rosie had arrived. No, she wasn't being nice to us. She was just being a creep because Mum had been so angry with her.

We both charged past Molly and rushed downstairs to see Rosie. Her bowl of spaghetti was super mega gross! It was a sort of horrible grey colour, and the currants looked exactly like dead flies... or even worse! We shoved it in the fridge, and dragged Rosie upstairs to help with the tape.

Emma has this totally fabulous stereo with a proper microphone and two tape decks, so we made one tape and then added more and more horrible noises on top. And we weren't spoiling anything that belonged to Emma: I was using all my own tapes. We were just borrowing her equipment.

Rosie whispered into the microphone, and Frankie did her best ever ghostly wails. I squeaked the door and moaned and groaned. Then we discovered that if we went a bit further away we could make it sound more echoey, so we opened the door and Rosie and I went down the stairs to make hollow footsteps.

Frankie waited until we were in position, and then switched on the microphone. As we stamped up the stairs she stamped down, making the most creepy ghastly chuckles. We were really enjoying ourselves, and Rosie was doing one final hideous cackle when—

Bang! Molly came storming out of her room.

"Can't you kids *shut up*?" she screeched. "You don't need to play your silly games on the stairs! It's bad enough having you shrieking and yelling in poor Emma's room!"

Of course the microphone recorded it all. We didn't bother answering her – we flew back to turn the microphone off, and then we slammed Emma's door.

"Doom and Disaster!" I said.

"Let's play it back," Frankie suggested. "Maybe Molly sounds like a hideous awful witch."

Rosie and I giggled, and we rewound the tape and pressed Play.

It was the most fantastical ghoulish tape ever – until Molly came on. She did sound dreadful. But not much like a witch.

"Shall we tape over it?" Rosie asked.

"No – let's leave it!" I said. "We'll tell Lyndz and Fliss we've got the only recording ever made of a horrible monster!"

We were in the kitchen making the green slime when Fliss and Lyndz arrived. Fliss knocked so politely we didn't hear her, but Lyndz gave the letter box a real hammering.

"Great!" I said when we were all in the kitchen. "The Sleepover Club's in action again! And we've got some real surprises for you... especially in the garden!"

Fliss was looking anxious already. She kept peering over her shoulder and jumping at the slightest noise, and now she gave a little squeak. "My mum says we're all to stay indoors," she said. "She says you don't know who might be watching the house to see if it's a good moment to get in."

I caught Frankie's eye, and we both burst

out laughing.

Fliss went very pink. "It's nothing to laugh about," she said.

"No," I said, "it's not that – we're laughing because Frankie and I spent *hours* outside today trying to get in and we couldn't! This house has to be the most burglar-proof house in the whole world!"

"Oh," Fliss said, and she began to look a bit better.

Then Frankie and I told the others about how Molly had refused to let us in and how Frankie's ice-cream head had been ruined.

When they'd heard the whole story, that settled it. We all made a vow of terrible revenge.

"We could haunt her all night," Frankie suggested.

"How about making her an apple-pie bed?" Lyndz giggled.

"Maybe we could tap on her window!" Rosie said.

Fliss went twitchy again. "But then we'd have to go outside!"

"Don't worry, we'll think of something! " I said, then I decided to change the subject. "Can we see your cake, Fliss?"

"Oh, yes! It's the best!" Fliss hurried out to the hall, and came back with a cake tin.

For once Fliss wasn't exaggerating. The cake *was* mega brilliant! It had two sorts of green swirled together, and there were jelly worms popping out of the icing and jelly spiders crouching round the bottom. We all ooohed and aaahed, and told Fliss how clever she was. Fliss smiled from ear to ear.

"I had some jelly worms left over," she said. "Here – I thought they might be useful."

"Great! We can put them in the slime," I said. "Where's your pizza, Lyndz?"

Lyndz grinned. "Wait and see!" she said.

"That's not fair!" Rosie said. "We've seen Fliss's cake!"

Lyndz just went on grinning and shook her head.

We couldn't hassle her any more because just then Mum came into the kitchen. "Are you lot still in here?" she said. "I need to get something ready for Dad – he's rushing in before his meeting—" She stopped when she saw the cake. "Goodness! That *is* clever!" Fliss blushed, and looked really pleased with herself again.

"It's nothing," she said in the sort of voice that means "Yes, I am very clever and I know I am!"

"It's OK, Mum," I said. "All we've got to do is bung the slime in the fridge and then we'll go upstairs."

"Fine," Mum said. "But don't forget—"

"Not to spoil anything of Emma's!" I finished her sentence for her.

We finished our stuff in the kitchen and galloped up the stairs to Emma's room.

"Come on," I said, "let's make ourselves some space here. Emma's away all weekend, so she'll never know. We can put everything back tomorrow."

"Isn't that spoiling things?" Fliss asked.

"No," I said. "It's *moving* things. If we move everything against the wall we can really spread out tonight. The way it is now we couldn't swing a cat."

Fliss giggled. "Poor cat!"

"I can swing a teddy!" Frankie said, and she whirled Emma's white bear round her head.

Crash! Emma's bedside lamp leapt off the table, and Rosie, Lyndz, Fliss and I cackled with laughter.

"Ooops!" Frankie got down on her hands and knees and picked it up again. "Maybe you were right, Kenny! There isn't any room to swing anything!"

We heaved and shoved and pushed the furniture right up against the walls, and piled Emma's clothes and shoes on one of the beds. Then we looked round.

"Wow!" Lyndz was dead impressed. "There's room to swing dozens of cats in here now!"

"Whoopee!" Frankie grabbed the white teddy again and swung it madly round her head. "Room to swing a teddy!"

Lyndz snatched up a green frog, and Rosie and Fliss fought over a fluffy bunny.

Fliss won, so Rosie pounced on a pink giraffe. I found a squashy elephant… and we swung them all round and round and round!

"Room to swing a jungle!" I yelled, and I let the elephant fly… and the elephant hit Rosie, and Rosie fell over onto Fliss, and Fliss whacked Lyndz with her fluffy bunny and Lyndz sent her green frog zooming across the room and—

Crash! The bedside lamp went flying for a second time.

This time the lamp broke. Seriously broke. Doom! The bottom bit was made of pink china (it was typical of Emma to have everything in prissy pink!) and the pink china was now in bits. The shade was bent too.

We went rather quiet for a moment as we looked at the wreckage.

"Sorry," Lyndz said.

"We're all to blame," Frankie said, and I nodded.

"If it's anyone's fault it's the frog's," Rosie said, and Frankie giggled. "Ground that frog!"

"Stop its pocket money!" I said.

"We could try and mend it," Fliss said. She was picking up the pieces. "Have you got any of that Super Glue stuff?"

"I don't know," I said. "There might be some in the kitchen. But Emma's bound to notice."

"Let's try anyway," Lyndz said.

"Mum'll still be cooking," I said. "We can go and look for the glue later. Anyway, there's no hurry. Emma's not back until Sunday night."

Down in the hall the telephone began to ring. Someone – or some*thing*! – must have heard what I'd just said, because two minutes later Molly came thundering up the stairs and stuck her head round the door. "Emma's got to come home tonight," she said with a great big silly grin on her face. "Jade's house has been burgled, and Emma can't stay after all!"

Molly looked round Emma's room at all the piled up furniture. "Ha! Looks like *you'll* be in big trouble now!" And she flounced out.

Emma coming home? We stared at each other.

Fliss put on her drama queen face. "I knew it!" she said, and she waved her arms. "It's because it's Friday 13th! Everything's bound to go wrong!"

CHAPTER SEVEN

"I'm going to ask Mum if it's true," I said, once I'd got over the shock. "The monster might have made it up – it's just the low-down kind of trick she likes to play."

As it turned out it *was* true – but it wasn't quite as bad as Molly had made it sound. Emma couldn't stay the night, but she and Jade had gone out to have a pizza, and Dad was going to collect her on the way back from his meeting.

"It's going to be quite late, so Emma may as well sleep in your room with Molly tonight," Mum said.

I heaved a huge sigh of relief – inside. Outside I just nodded. "OK," I said.

Mum gave me a suspicious sort of look. "I hope you haven't been making a mess up there," she said. "Molly says you've been moving furniture."

"We only moved things a little," I said. "And we do that in my room."

"Fine." Mum went on stirring something in a saucepan. "Molly and I are eating with Dad, so you lot can do your feasting on green cake afterwards in peace."

"Thanks, Mum, you're the best," I said, and gave her a hug.

I was going back up the stairs when I heard Dad coming in. I gave a quick wave over the banisters, and then shot back into Emma's room to tell the others not to panic – yet!

"We can sort the room out in the morning," I said.

Fliss was peering out of the window. "I'm sure I heard a strange noise," she said. "Do you think there's someone down there?" She was looking twitchy again.

"I expect it's Dad," I said. "He's just come home."

"Oh," Fliss said, but she didn't sound very convinced.

"Let's go and see!" Frankie said, and she made a face at me behind Fliss's back, and mouthed, "*Blood trail*!"

"Oh no!" Fliss squeaked. "We ought to stay inside!"

"It'll be OK with all of us," Lyndz said, and she grinned. "What burglar would take on the Sleepover Club?"

Even Fliss smiled a little. "I still don't think we shou—" she began, but she didn't sound so certain.

"Come on!" Lyndz grabbed her hand. "We can make sure it's all clear down there while it's still light! We'll check out the bushes!"

"Only a mini burglar could hide in your garden," Rosie said.

"That's it!" I said. "The burglar's only sixty centimetres tall – and that's why no one's found him yet!"

We were halfway down the stairs when Frankie suddenly stopped. "Sssh!" she said. "We sound like a herd of elephants! From now on we've got to go on tiptoe!"

"Tippytoe! Tippytoe! Hunting burglars! Here we go!" giggled Lyndz, and we got in a line and tiptoed down the rest of the stairs and out of the front door. (We made sure we left it on the latch this time. Frankie and I weren't taking any more chances!)

It was beginning to get dark as we crept round the side of the house. Frankie was in front, then me, then Lyndz, then Rosie, and then Fliss.

"Tippytoe! Tippytoe! Tippytoe!" sang Lyndz, and we all tiptoed in time down the path, until—

"Look!" Frankie did her mega-thrill, over-the-top acting voice and stopped dead on the path.

We all crashed into each other, and somehow Fliss ended up at the front – so she saw the trail of blood before Lyndz or Rosie. And she screamed…

I think the rest of us were as frightened by Fliss's scream as she was frightened by the blood. I know my heart gave a huge walloping leap inside my chest, and I heard Lyndz gasp beside me. When someone really truly screams for real, it's not a nice noise at all – it's *really* scary! And then Fliss turned and she *ran* back into the house, and of course we all tore after her.

If it had been me I think I'd have headed straight for the grown-ups, but Fliss didn't – luckily for us. She zoomed up to Emma's room, and when we got there she was shaking all over and trying to stuff her pyjamas into her bag.

"Fliss, what are you doing?" I asked.

She looked up, and her face was a horrible colour – completely grey-green. "I want to go home," she said. "I saw blood all over your path! I want my mum! I'm scared!"

I looked at Frankie, and Frankie looked at me. "I'm really sorry, Fliss," I said. "It wasn't blood – it was just raspberry juice from Frankie's pudding."

"It melted when we were shut outside," Frankie said. "And it seemed a pity to waste it all – so we trailed it round the path."

"Are you sure it wasn't blood?" Fliss still looked like a frightened rabbit, but at least she'd stopped shaking. She'd stopped trying to pack her pyjamas, too.

I suddenly remembered what Dad had told me about people who'd had a terrible fright. You should keep them warm, and if there's no chance of them having any kind of internal injury, you should give them a warm drink.

"Hang on!" I said. "Frankie, put my duvet round Fliss!" and I rushed off downstairs.

Molly and Mum were just finishing eating, and Dad had made a pot of tea. Just the thing!

"Can I take a cup of tea up to Fliss?" I said. "She's – she's a bit cold."

"I thought I heard you go outside," Mum said. "Don't go out again, though – it's getting dark now."

I wondered why they hadn't heard Fliss

scream. The noise was still ringing inside my head. Probably Molly had been bleating on about some boring thing she was doing at school – or maybe they thought it was on the TV. I could hear it mumbling away in the sitting room.

I poured out the tea, shoved in a big spoonful of sugar, and got out of the door as fast as I could before anyone asked me any awkward questions.

Upstairs, Fliss was much better. She was wrapped up in my duvet, and Lyndz was fussing round her in just the way Fliss likes best. She drank the tea, and her face went back to its normal colour.

"It's a good thing we didn't have time to make a body!" Frankie said cheerfully. "Fliss would have had a hundred fits then!"

"Mum says I'm very sensitive," Fliss said, sounding really pleased about it. Then she shivered again. "The blood did look real, though!"

"I never got a chance to see it properly," Rosie said in a disappointed voice, and that made us all laugh.

There was a knock on the door. "Kitchen's clear!" Dad said, and we heard him stomping off into my parent's room. I guessed he was going to get ready for his meeting.

"I say it's food time!" shouted Lyndz. "Can I go down and put my pizza in the oven first? You lot stay up here for two minutes – I don't want anyone seeing it until it's ready!"

We counted one hundred and twenty hippopotamuses to give Lyndz time to sort out her pizza, and then we couldn't wait any longer. We rushed downstairs to sort out our ghoulish grub. Fliss still seemed to be suffering from shock, and she jumped a mile when Rosie dropped a spoon. I wished she'd get back to normal soon. I was feeling a little guilty that we'd scared her half to death!

When Lyndz finally pulled the pizza out of the oven we all gasped again. Usually Frankie is the one who makes pizzas – her dad is famous for them – and Lyndz's pizza wasn't fab in the way Frankie's are. But it *was* fabulously gross. For a start it was green – a muddy, been buried for ages sort of green. It was folded over in half, so the two edges looked a bit like horrible ghoulish lips... and there were fingers sticking out! Horrible, drooping, floppy, *shiny pink* fingers, with oozy blood dribbling out between each of them. (Actually they were sausages, but they really looked like fingers.)

We all shouted *yuck*! together – it was *so* brilliant!

We carried all the food upstairs; during sleepovers, we always eat our food in the bedroom – it's much more fun. The green slime wibbled and wobbled like mad; I'd filled the bowl rather full, but we just about managed not to spill it. At least, not much of it – a little slimed its way out when Rosie tried to open the door with one hand and hold the bowl with the other. It looked as if a large slug had been trying to ooze its way into Emma's room!

We put the food on the floor, snuggled into our sleeping bags and turned the lights off. Then we pulled out our torches. Have you ever eaten like that? It's awesome! Although you don't always see when things get spilt.

"Let's put our horror tape on!" Frankie suggested.

"Great idea," I said.

We had to put the light back on to see what we were doing with the stereo, but we turned it off again after I'd pressed Play.

The tape had only been on for a second when Fliss jumped up. "I want the light back on," she said, scrambling through all the food to the light switch. Then she turned the tape off. "It's HORRIBLE!" she said, shivering.

Sometimes I think Fliss is the biggest wimp I've ever met. We tried everything we could think of, but there was no way we could persuade her to let us put the tape on in the dark. She said she didn't mind the torches, but no tape. If we wanted the tape *she* wanted the light on. In the end we gave in. We didn't play the tape.

The food was some of the best ever.

Rosie's grey spaghetti was kind of chewy, but it didn't matter. Lyndz said it was a bowl of horror worms and we could only eat them by sucking them up! We took it in turn slurping them out of the bowl and we slurped the slime as well. It was wicked! The pizza didn't just look awesome, it tasted scrummy, too. We'd saved the cake for the very last. Fliss began to smile a lot more when we got near the time to cut the cake!

"We should each cut a slice and wish," she said. "Then maybe we won't have any more bad luck."

We all agreed that was a great idea, and I handed Fliss the knife. "You go first," I said, and Fliss held it over the green jelly-worm icing.

"I wish—" she began, but didn't get any further.

"Laura! I want you and all your friends down here *at once*!"

It was Dad. He was shouting up the stairs, and he sounded *mad*.

CHAPTER EIGHT

We went out to the hall, and there was Dad. At least, it had to be Dad because the thing standing there had Dad's voice and it was Dad's height – but otherwise you couldn't really tell because it was snow white. Or rather flour white… and I knew it was flour because he was holding the cat hot-water bottle in his hand. He looked incredibly weird – I mean, I knew it was my Dad, but he looked like a ghost!

The others didn't know what to think. Fliss stared with her eyes out on stalks. Rosie and Frankie and Lyndz began to giggle

– but they soon stopped when they saw my dad's face. If this was a ghost, it was a very, very *angry* ghost!

Oooooops! I couldn't help thinking that we were having enough bad luck to last us for years and years…

"Is this one of your ridiculous Friday 13th tricks?" Dad roared. "I was in the kitchen, just about to go to a *very* important meeting – and *whoomp*! I get attacked by a flying hot-water bottle. One minute I'm standing minding my own business and finishing a quiet cup of tea, and the next – *furry cats come zooming out of cupboards*. And my best suit is ruined!"

I opened my mouth to say it was all my fault, and none of the others knew about it – but I never got the chance. Just then Mum came out of the sitting room – she saw Dad and she began to laugh. Actually laugh!

"I'm sorry," she said, "but you do look funny. Whatever happened?"

Dad tried to look dignified, but it wasn't easy. He waved the furry hot-water bottle in the air. "It's one of Laura's silly tricks!" he said. "Or one of her friend's! They're all as bad as each other! I was looking for the shoe polish and this" – he waved the cat again – "flew out of the top cupboard in the kitchen and covered me with some kind of white dust!"

I opened my mouth again, but Mum got in there first.

"Oh no!" she said, and she began to dust Dad down. "Do you know, I think for once Kenny's not to blame? I think it's *my* fault! I put that cat away ages ago. I don't think Kenny even knew where it was – did you?" And Mum turned to me.

Well – what would you have done? Would you have leapt forward and said "No, it was me! I did it!"? I did dither for a milli-second. Then I said, "I didn't know it was there until today." Which *was* true... and I was thinking I'd got away with it when Mum suddenly stopped brushing.

"Just a moment," she said. "This isn't dust. It's flour – I'm sure it is!" Both she and

Dad swivelled round to look at me. I could feel myself going pink. Time to own up....

"It jumped out at me this morning," I said. "I was looking in the kitchen cupboard and it did exactly the same thing to me. It scared me off my stool!"

"So you thought you'd put it back," Mum said. "And give it a little extra dusting... so when it jumped out again it would be even better!"

Sometimes I think Mum is a mind-reader. I nodded.

"*Humph*," Mum said, and she looked at Dad. She still had a twinkle in her eye, but Dad didn't. Not at all. He was grumbling away like a volcano – I hoped he wasn't going to explode *too* loudly.

"It's all very well playing silly games," he said. "But my suit's filthy, and I'm going to be late if I don't hurry. I think we'd better talk about this tomorrow, Laura."

"Sorry, Dad," I said, and he stomped off into the kitchen.

Mum must have been able to brush the

worst of the flour off because I heard the car leave about two minutes later.

The others and I hurried back to our interrupted cake. As soon as we'd shut the door it struck me how funny Dad had looked, and I began to giggle. The others started, too, and when I told them how the furry hot-water bottle had scared me silly before breakfast they laughed even more.

"Your Dad looked like a real ghost!" Lyndz chortled, and she rolled over and over on the floor.

"We should have asked him up to eat horror worms with us!" Rosie cackled. "Whooo! Whoooo! Whooooo! All the worms would have run away!"

"If he walked round the streets like that he'd scare the burglar into the middle of next week!" hooted Frankie.

"I'm glad that furry thing didn't jump out when we were in the kitchen," Fliss said. "I think I'd have died of fright!" She probably would have, too, knowing Fliss!

We sat down again to cut the cake, but we

were all really giggly. You know what it's like when anything at all makes you laugh, even if it's not really funny? Well, we were like that – even Fliss. We waved jelly worms at each other, and we made the jelly spiders plop into the remains of the green slime… and we began to tell ghost stories. We sat in the dark and made them up as we went along, and our ideas became more and more ridiculous.

Lyndz started off the story; she said she'd heard that there was a headless woman who walked round and round the house at midnight where a Dreadful Deed had been done.

Then Rosie said that it must be a house near where she lived, because there were often strange wailings and howlings in the night. She said there were two dogs who howled, but they didn't sound like dogs at all.

Frankie went next and said that in the old days people believed evil spirits could change into dogs, and this was what these dogs were. We took it in turns to describe what they looked like – "glowing red eyes!" and "slobbering jaws!" and "huge, ginormous teeth!"

"And then," Frankie said, and she made her voice go very deep and scary, "one of the monster dogs began creeping and crawling along the road... and it saw—"

"Molly the Monster!" I interrupted. "And both dogs turned round and ran away as fast as they could go!" And we all burst into giggles all over again.

"We still haven't played that tape," I said at last. "Fliss, if we put the light on can we play it? Only I must warn you, there's a real live monster at the end!"

Fliss pulled a long face and looked as if she was about to say no again, but we all pleaded with her until she had to give in.

"All right," she said reluctantly. "As long as the light's on."

I squirmed out of my sleeping bag and began crawling across the floor to the light switch. Of course I had to climb over everyone else – and there was some furious wriggling as I wormed my way across the floor.

"I'm a *horror* worm!" I hissed. "And I'm coming to get you!"

The sleeping-bag worms wriggled this way and that as I pounced. I found knobbly worms and squashy worms and…

Yuck! I put my hand right in the slimiest squishiest thing I'd ever felt. I didn't have time to say anything, though, because a sleeping-bag worm grabbed me by the ankles and pulled me back along the floor… and the slimy stuff came with me. I tried to grab something, and there was a muffled shriek as my horrible slimy hand met Rosie's face.

Two screams in one night! Luckily Rosie doesn't scream as loudly as Fliss – and she had a mouthful of slime as well. But it was still mega-creepy.

Fliss and Lyndz and Frankie sat bolt upright, and Fliss said, "What's happening?" in a quivery voice.

"Everyone be quiet," I said. "You'll get my mum up here."

I found the light switch and turned it on.

Rosie had green slime on her face, and I had it all over my hand. The carpet had a green smear all along where I'd been dragged – but at least we knew it was only jelly. It hadn't felt like jelly when I put my hand in it, though; I suppose that's what happens when you're in the dark.

I took Rosie to the bathroom to clean herself up, and while I was there I grabbed a towel. The carpet looked better after we'd rubbed it a bit.

"It's only wet," Frankie said. "After all, that's all jelly slime is – mostly water. It'll have dried by the morning."

Just to be on the safe side we moved the rest of the food onto one of the beds out of our way.

"Did you see the moonlight when we were in the bathroom?" Rosie asked as we climbed back into our sleeping bags. "We ought to open the curtains. It's really bright!"

"What about the tape?" Fliss asked.

"I'll put it on in a minute," I said. "Let's look at the moonlight first."

We opened the curtains and turned the light off. Rosie was quite right. The moon *was* very bright – it was almost like having the light on.

"Open the window," Frankie said. "You can see everything out there!"

We opened the window, and peered out. It was very quiet outside, and the moonlight made long shadows across the path.

"It looks magical!" Fliss said, wistfully.

We were quite quiet for a moment or two while we looked outside. And then we saw it. Something – someone – was climbing very carefully over the fence. The fence into *my garden*.

CHAPTER NINE

You'd have thought one of us would have screamed – especially Fliss. But we didn't. It was very strange. Somehow the idea of a burglar was much *much* more scary than the real thing. Or perhaps it was because we were safely inside a big house with lots of locks on all the doors, and Mum was downstairs. The burglar looked quite small and skinny, too – not at all massive and thuggish.

"Is it really a burglar?" Rosie whispered.

"I think so," I whispered back.

The burglar rubbed his hands on his

trousers as he came away from the fence. We saw him look at the house – *my house*! and then move very softly through the plants and bushes towards the path. It was like watching a cat, or some other night animal.

"We ought to tell Mum," I whispered, but I didn't get up. After all, he hadn't done anything yet. He was just walking towards the path…

Yowl! Eeeeeeeeeeeeeeeeek! Owwwwwwllll llllllllllie Wowlie!

It was our horror tape, and it was playing at the sort of volume that cracks your ears open and splits your head. I leapt a million miles in the air – but that was nothing to the way the burglar jumped. He jumped as if someone had given him a zillion megawatt electric shock, spun round – and fell flat on his back with a massive *thwack*!

We were frozen rigid. We hung out of the window staring.

"Is he dead?" Frankie whispered.

"I'd better get Mum!" I said, and hurtled

off down the stairs.

Mum was halfway up the stairs, anyway. I guess she couldn't have missed the noise – which was still blaring out. She could see at once that something was up, though – and when I blurted out, "Mum! Mum! There's a burglar dead on the path!" she flew to the phone.

Have you ever had to dial 999? I've always wanted to – and now Mum was doing it! She was really calm and cool as well. I'd have probably forgotten my address, my telephone number *and* my name!

"Right," Mum said as she snapped down the receiver. "Where's this burglar?"

"You mustn't go outside!" I gasped. "Supposing he was only winded? He might hurt us!"

"I wasn't going to," Mum said. "We'll look out of the window."

Our tape suddenly went quiet. Frankie came to the top of the stairs. "He's still there!" she whispered down. "He's moved a little – but he hasn't got up!"

Molly burst into the hall. "What's going on?" she said. She glared at me. "More of your silly baby Friday 13th games, I suppose."

"Molly," Mum said, "just go back into the sitting room. There's nothing to worry about."

I was so proud of my mum! She was still dead calm. Ferocious burglars were lurking in our garden, and she was acting as cool as a cucumber!

Molly gave me a furious look and disappeared.

When we looked out of the dining-room window I could see the burglar much better. He really did look small.

"He's not wearing a mask," I said.

"No," Mum said. "And he's not wearing a black-and-white striped top or carrying a bag on his back marked SWAG, either!"

The burglar started to move. He tried to sit up, but there seemed to be something wrong with his leg.

"Dear me," Mum said suddenly. "He must

be badly hurt! Look! He's sitting in a pool of blood! Poor man! I'd better go and see if I can help him!"

"Oh!" I said, and a massive flash of understanding zoomed into my brain. I knew why the burglar had fallen over. He'd slipped – in our trail.

"Hang on, Mum!" I said. "It isn't *real* blood. It's the melted stuff from Frankie's pudding. Rather a lot of it got – er – spilt on the path. That's why he slipped!"

I think Mum was about to say something when we heard the police cars.

DEE – DAW – DEE – DAW – DEE – DAW

I've heard them hundreds of times before, but this time was different. This time they were coming to *our* house! The burglar heard it, too, and he tried to get up again – but he couldn't.

Mum went to the front door. "Laura," she said, "go back upstairs."

"But Mum—" I protested.

"Go!" Mum said, and when she talks in that tone of voice I do as I'm told. Fast!

Rosie, Lyndz, Frankie and Fliss grabbed me as I came through the door. They all started speaking at once.

"We heard the police car!"

"Look – he's trying to move!"

"Here they come! I can see the lights!"

"Why did he fall over? Is he all right?"

And then four policemen came charging into our garden with the biggest torches you ever saw – and one of them was kneeling by the burglar checking to see where he was hurt.

"There's a lot of blood around here, Sarge," a big policeman said. "Where d'you think it's come from?"

Another policeman bent down and peered with his torch at the path. Frankie and I held our breath. Our trail of blood glistened very red in the beam of light. Then the policeman stood up, and we could see him grinning. His teeth flashed in the moonlight. "That's not blood, Sarge. It's jam – or something very like it!"

"What's going on? Is anyone hurt? I'm a

doctor!" It was Dad, hurrying to the scene of the crime. The whole thing was exactly like something on TV! And we were up at our window watching it for real!

"Well, sir – if you'd be kind enough to look at this young fellow," a policeman said.

We could see Dad checking the burglar by the light of the police torches.

"Hmm," said Dad. "Broken ankle, I'd say. You'd be best off getting him to a hospital for an X-ray." Then he suddenly leant forward, and peered at the burglar. "Hang on a moment. I know you! You were hanging around my surgery last week! And I saw you trying the car doors in the car park!"

The sergeant looked excited. "Could you swear to that, sir?"

"I certainly could," Dad said. "But what's going on? What are you all doing in my garden?"

I was dying to yell out that it was the burglar, and that we'd caught him – but I didn't. Mum was out there now as well, and I thought it might be best if she explained things. I went on watching with the others.

At least, we went on watching for another minute, and then the light switched on behind us – and there was Emma.

No burglar could ever be as terrifying as Emma in a really furious mood – and this time she wasn't just really furious. She was mega mega *mega* furious. She shouted and yelled and screamed at us, and called us all sorts of names. Molly couldn't resist joining in, and every time Emma slowed down Molly would point out some other thing that we'd done – like the slimy wet patch on the carpet, or the broken lamp, or the cake crumbs everywhere, or the tape in her stereo.

We didn't say anything. Emma wouldn't have listened if we had.

GOODBYE

Mum and Dad finally waved the police goodbye, and came back in. The burglar went off with the police in their car.

As soon as Mum was in earshot Emma started shrieking at her. "Come and look!" she yelled. "Come and see what they've done to my room! She *knows* she's not allowed in here – and all her horrible little friends are here, too, and they've *wrecked* my room!"

Molly just stood there and sniggered.

Dad and Mum appeared in the doorway, and Dad put his arm round Emma's shoulders – but he gave us a huge wink.

"They'll clear it all up in the morning," he said. "I know they get daft ideas in their heads – and some are dafter than others – but tonight's a little bit different. You see, your sister and her friends have caught a burglar!" And he gently shooed Emma and Molly away.

Well you'd think that we'd have got some kind of medal for catching a burglar, wouldn't you? Or a reward. In all the books you read there are always huge rewards. But us? We ended up spending the next morning cleaning up Emma's room!

We did get our picture in *The Mercury* though. A reporter came and took our photo all together, grinning like monkeys. He asked us if we often played at catching burglars and loads of other questions. Then of course we all got really excited about how we were going to become local celebrities, given special treatment wherever we went and generally made a fuss of, but when the paper came out it sounded as if we were about six. Emma and Molly teased me about it for ages.

Yes, Emma is finally speaking to me again. She even apologised for calling the others horrible! She's OK really. She doesn't hold grudges, unlike Molly. Mind you I do have to buy her a new lamp and pay to have the carpet cleaned. Mum's taking the money out of my allowance – she said it was only fair.

We had to scrub the garden path, too. I thought the police might want to see all the footprints going up and down, but as Dad said, what was the point? They'd caught the burglar. So – it was soapy water and scrubbing brushes for the Sleepover Club. Actually, we had quite a lot of fun. It got very bubbly…

And at least we weren't grounded, so we can have another sleepover really soon – I'll look forward to seeing you there. I've got a feeling it may not be as eventful as Friday 13th was – but with the Sleepover Club you never can tell!

P.S. Just in case you were wondering, I've

come back to tell you. Or maybe you've already guessed who switched on the tape – and gave the burglar the fright of his life? I didn't. I couldn't believe it when Frankie told me. It was Fliss! There may be some hope for her after all…

See ya!

Sleepover Girls Go Camping

by Fiona Cummings

Collins

An imprint of HarperCollins*Publishers*

CHAPTER ONE

Don't you just love children's playgrounds? I do and I love the swings best of all. There's nothing better than flying right up into the air and whooshing back. I think everyone should go on a swing once in a while, just to clear their heads. Grown-ups as well. Especially grown-ups.

My friends think I'm crazy. They say:

"Lyndz, anybody would think *Ben* was taking *you* to the playground, not the other way round."

In case you've forgotten, Ben's my four-year-old brother. He's a bit wild. He'd much rather be bashing people over the head with his pretend sword than playing on the swings. Still, my baby brother, Spike, enjoys going to the playground, so I quite often take him. Not today though. Today I'm meeting the rest of the Sleepover Club. You can come too, if you like. In fact you've got to come, because I want to tell you all about our latest adventure. It was mega-cool.

You remember that we all belong to the same Brownie Pack, don't you? Well, just over a month ago, Brown Owl told us about this special camp she was arranging during the summer holidays.

"It's for those of you who'll soon be going up to Guides," she said.

"That's us!" said Rosie and I together.

"There's going to be a special four-day 'under canvas' camp at Foxton Glen at the beginning of August. It's a fun way to get you used to the kind of things that Guides do," Brown Owl continued.

"Cool!" shouted Kenny. "We can leave Brownies to the babies!"

"I heard that, Laura McKenzie!" said Brown Owl, scowling at Kenny.

Kenny scowled right back at her. If there's one thing she hates it's being called by her proper name. 'Laura' is way too girlie for her!

"What will we be doing at the camp?" asked Frankie, quickly changing the subject before Kenny got too out of control.

Frankie's our sort of unofficial Sleepover Club leader. She's so sensible you see.

"Well, you'll be helping to put up your own tents for a start, then there's abseiling, canoeing, a climbing wall, archery—"

"Wicked!" laughed Kenny. "It's going to be cooler than a fridge full of Magnum ice creams!" She was so hyper, I thought she was going to start bouncing round the room at any minute.

I turned to Fliss, who was sitting next to me. "What's she like!" I laughed. But then I saw Fliss's face. She was not a happy bunny. "What's up with you?" I said.

"I hate all those things," she moaned.

9

"You know, abseiling and stuff – it's just not me!"

She was right there. Fliss is not really an outdoorsy kind of girl. Give her a bottle of nail varnish and a pile of magazines and she's in heaven. Shinning down the side of a building on a rope – well, that's more like Fliss's idea of hell. She's very clean is Fliss, and strictly one for her home comforts.

I couldn't help feeling sorry for Fliss. The rest of us were getting all excited about the idea of going away on this special camp and you could tell that she was starting to feel really left out. And that's another thing about Fliss – she hates to be left out of anything.

"How much will it cost?" Rosie asked Brown Owl in her quiet voice.

The rest of us looked at each other worriedly. We know that Rosie's a bit conscious about money since her father left home. But seeing as he coughed up for our trip to Spain, we hoped there'd be no reason why he shouldn't do it again for the camp.

"Well, I'm just finalising details about that," Brown Owl told her, "but it should be quite reasonable. We're hoping that Brownies from the 12th Cuddington pack will be joining us. And the more people there are, the more people there'll be to share the cost."

"Oh great!" piped up a voice. "Our friends Regina and Amanda belong to 12th, don't they, Emily?"

The voice belonged to the horrible Emma Hughes. She and Emily Berryman are our sworn enemies, the M&Ms. Just for one lovely moment I'd forgotten they were in the same Brownie pack as us. And because they're the same age as the rest of us, they'll be moving up to Guides soon, too. That meant that the Gruesome Twosome would be coming to the camp. Suddenly it didn't seem quite so great after all.

"Now, could all those older Brownies who are interested in going to Foxton Glen please put up their hands. Just so I've got some idea of numbers," said Brown Owl.

Kenny, Frankie, Rosie and I shot up our hands. So did the awful M&Ms and their friend Alana 'Banana' Palmer, plus a few more girls.

"Felicity, I don't see your hand up," said Snowy Owl, who is also Fliss's auntie Jill.

Fliss did a real cherry. Even her blonde hair looked as though it was blushing.

"I, er– I'm not sure," she stammered.

The M&Ms sniggered behind their hands.

"Oh Felicity, I'm sure you'll love it," Snowy Owl told her. "Besides, all your friends want to go. Won't you feel left out if you miss all the fun?"

Smart move, Snowy Owl – if anything was going to make Fliss change her mind, that would do it! Fliss raised her hand very slowly.

"All right!" shouted Kenny, leaping to her feet. "It'll be mega! Just think of all those sleepovers we can have!"

"I'll have a letter ready for your parents by next week's meeting, which will give details of the cost," explained Brown Owl.

"Then those of you who decide to go must bring your money the following week."

Well, you can imagine what we were like for the next week, can't you?

"This is painful!" sniffed Fliss on Saturday afternoon. We were in Frankie's bedroom, talking about the camp, as usual. "I'm sick of you going on about that stupid camp. Can't we talk about something else?"

"Like make-up?" I suggested.

"Or clothes?" asked Frankie.

"Or what about Ryan Scott?" asked Kenny, pretending to kiss Frankie's teddy, Stanley.

"Shut up!" snapped Fliss.

"Maybe you shouldn't come after all," said Rosie. "But what would you do all by yourself while we're away?"

Fliss looked really anxious, like she hadn't thought about that. She paused for a moment and then said, "Well, what do you have to do at this camp? They don't make you do loads of frightening things, do they?"

"No, of course they don't," Rosie reassured her. "Tiff used to be in the Guides and she said the camps are really wicked."

Tiff is Rosie's older sister.

"They make this mega-big camp fire," she continued, "and everyone sits round it and sings. And sometimes you actually cook your food on the fire."

That sounded a bit like a recipe for disaster for us – The Sleepover Club are hopeless when it comes to cooking – but it did sound like a laugh.

"What else do you do?" asked Fliss. "You can't spend all your time round the fire."

"There are nature trails and stuff," Kenny told her. "And on the last night there's a sort of concert and everyone has to perform in front of the others."

We all stared at her in amazement.

"What are you looking at?" she snapped. "I've been asking Molly the Monster about it. She does have some uses. She went to Foxton Glen on an 'under canvas' camp last summer."

It was a miracle that Kenný had managed to ask her sister Molly anything without World War III starting. To say that they don't get on is like saying that Ronan Keating is gorgeous: it's kind of stating the obvious.

"So it's not all big and scary then?" asked Fliss. She definitely looked a zillion times brighter now.

"No way!" laughed Frankie. "Guides do the same kinds of things as Brownies, only they're a bit more adventurous. And I bet you'll be able to think of something really awesome to perform at the concert!"

Fliss grinned this big grin. "It does sound kind of cool," she laughed. "I thought there might be one of those awful assault courses, and I'm dead scared of those. You know, crawling over those nets and through all that mud and everything. Urgh!" She did this big dramatic shiver. "But that's just crazy, right? They won't have one of those, will they? Because if they do, there's absolutely no way that I'm going to this camp."

We all looked at each other.

"What's up with you lot?" asked Fliss.

"Nothing," said Rosie and Frankie quickly.

"Assault course!" guffawed Kenny loudly. "I wish!"

"Hic!" I gulped. You can always rely on me to get hiccups when things get a bit awkward.

"Hey, Fliss, can you go down to the kitchen and get a glass of water for Lyndz?" asked Frankie. She started to knead my hand with her thumbs – a trick that usually cures my hiccups.

As soon as we were sure that Fliss was downstairs, we all started to talk at once.

"But there *is* an assault course at Foxton Glen, isn't there?" asked Frankie.

"Yep and Tiff says it's pretty awesome, too," nodded Rosie.

"And isn't there an Assault Course Challenge at the end of the camp?" asked Frankie again.

"There sure is," confirmed Kenny. "Monster Features told me all about it. Teams race against each other and there's a trophy for first prize and everything. Molly's team came second, so we've got to win when we go."

"But… hic… Fliss won't go… hic… if she finds out… hic… about that," I said between hiccups.

"Well we won't tell her then, will we?" decided Kenny.

"We won't tell who what?" asked Fliss rushing in with my glass of water. I took it from her and started to drink.

"We won't, um, tell Brown Owl that Kenny snores," said Frankie quickly.

As soon as she said that I took a big gulp of water and started to choke. Kenny started to slap me on the back – really hard.

"Yes, because someone who went to camp with Molly snored," Kenny told Fliss, "and Brown Owl made them pitch their tent right in the middle of the wood, miles away from the others."

Fliss's eyes became enormous. "Seriously?" she asked anxiously. "I'd hate that. You won't tell her about Kenny's snoring, will you?"

"Of course we won't!" Frankie reassured her.

"Um, Kenny, you can stop hitting me now," I yelped. "I'm not choking anymore. And my hiccups have gone!"

That was the last time we spoke about the camp before the next Brownie meeting. We figured that if we didn't mention it at all, then Fliss wouldn't find out about the assault course at Foxton Glen. She'd sounded deadly serious about not going if there was one, and it would be awful to go away without her. The Sleepover Club tends to do everything together, and having a sleepover without one of us there would feel too weird. It was going to be a real challenge to keep the assault course a secret from Fliss, but of course it was crucial that she didn't find out.

CHAPTER TWO

The following week, the rest of us waited for Fliss outside the church hall before our Brownie meeting.

When she appeared, Kenny hissed, "Right, not a word about the assault course!"

Fliss walked over to us. She looked in a real mood. "I suppose Brown Owl will be going on about that stupid camp again," she said crossly.

"Well, a 'Hello, how are you?' would have been nice!" joked Kenny.

"And there's no need to sound so enthusiastic about the camp!" laughed

Frankie. "We wouldn't want you to actually enjoy yourself now, would we?"

"I'm not sure that I'm going to go," Fliss said.

"What?" we all yelled.

"But you said you *were*, last time we talked about it." Rosie sounded exasperated.

"Yes, I know, but I want to find out whether or not there's an assault course there," explained Fliss. "And I can't ask Auntie Jill because Mum says that she's on a course from work or something. She won't be coming to Brownies for the next few weeks."

"That's a pity!" said Kenny innocently.

If Fliss didn't have the chance to ask Snowy Owl about the assault course, she probably wouldn't find out about it until we were safely at camp. And by then it would be too late!

"I don't understand what the big deal is about an assault course anyway," I said. "I mean, even if there *is* one – OUCH!" I suddenly fell to the ground.

"Whoops, sorry, Lyndz. I think I must

have tripped you up," said Kenny. As she bent to help me up, she hissed in my ear, "I told you not to mention the assault course."

"I know – but—" I spluttered.

"Goodness, Lyndsey, that was quite a tumble. Are you all right?" Brown Owl asked, as she ushered us into the hall.

I nodded and gave Kenny a dirty look.

At the start of our meetings Brown Owl always runs through everything we're going to do. When she mentioned the camp and the letters to take home we all held our breath. We were sure that Fliss was going to ask her about the assault course. But Brown Owl said that we'd a lot to get through and sort of hurried us into our sixes to work on our Season's Badge, so Fliss didn't get the chance.

As we're not all in the same six, we didn't meet up again properly until the end of the meeting when Brown Owl was handing out the letters about the camp.

"Don't forget – I need your parent's

permission slips and your money by next week," she reminded us.

Emma Hughes and Emily Berryman jostled and pushed us to make sure that they were the first ones to get their sweaty little paws on the letters.

"Pathetic!" spat Kenny.

"We'll see who's pathetic when we beat you in the Challenge at the end of the camp!" sneered Emma Hughes.

"Oh yeah? We'll see about that!" retorted Kenny.

The M&Ms tossed their hair and stalked away.

Fliss, who was next to me at the back of the group, asked anxiously, "What Challenge?"

"Um, I'm not sure," I said quickly. "It's probably who sings the best songs round the camp fire or something."

"Oh great," said Fliss. "I love singing like that, we'll probably win the Challenge – easy!"

"Oh you think so, do you, Miss Prissy-Knickers?" snarled Emma Hughes, who had suddenly appeared out of nowhere. "Well you'd better start practising. I wouldn't have thought a weed like you would be much good at—"

"I've got your letters," Frankie said loudly. She quickly thrust two letters about the camp at Fliss and me, and stood between us and the M&Ms.

"Crikey, Fliss, look at the time!" said Rosie who had joined us. "Your mum'll be wondering where we are!"

"Better run along to mummikins!" mimicked the Gruesome Twosome.

Fliss went bright red.

"You should go, too," shouted Kenny. "It's getting windy now and we wouldn't want you to take a wrong turn on your broomsticks!"

We all screamed with laughter and, linking arms, we ran as fast as we could out of the hall and down the path.

Fliss's mum and my dad were waiting for us outside. Rosie went with Fliss and I'd arranged to give Kenny and Frankie a lift home. When we'd waved goodbye to the others, the three of us piled into Dad's van and Frankie pretended to collapse in a heap.

"Phew, that was close!" she said, wiping her brow dramatically.

"I know!" I squealed, "I couldn't believe it when you got into a row with the M&Ms, Kenny. I thought Fliss was bound to suss something out."

"Then when the M&Ms had a go at her about winning the Challenge," giggled Kenny, "and she thought they were talking about singing!"

We all exploded into laughter.

"Do you think she's going to find out about the assault course before the camp?" I asked when we'd calmed down.

"I hope not," said Frankie.

"There's only a week before we have to give in the forms. And once she's paid her money, Fliss can't really back down, can she?" reasoned Kenny.

"We'll have to avoid the M&Ms, though," said Frankie. "They could easily mention the

Assault Course Challenge again, and that would completely finish Fliss off!"

When we'd dropped Frankie and Kenny off, I started to panic. It wouldn't be easy avoiding the M&Ms because we're all in the same class at school. The camp was planned for the summer holidays but we had one week at school before the end of term. The only way we could be sure that the M&Ms wouldn't mention anything to Fliss was if we kidnapped her and kept her in a cupboard. The thought was tempting but a bit impossible. We would just have to stay on our toes and be extra wary of them.

For that last week, every time we saw Emma Hughes or Emily Berryman, we bundled Fliss out of the way. Or we started to talk extra loudly, so that even if they did say anything Fliss wouldn't be able to hear it.

On the last day of term we all went a bit wild. We seemed to spend more time outside than we did in the classroom. We were too hyper to work and even Mrs

Weaver, our teacher, knew it. The M&Ms seemed to be spending a lot of time leaping over obstacles – a bench, the rubbish bin, Ryan Scott.

"Sad!" said Kenny loudly as she passed them.

"You won't be saying that when we beat you in the—" started Emma Hughes, and we all knew what she was going to say next.

"Hey, Fliss, look!" Rosie dragged Fliss away.

"Daisy chains!" screamed Frankie, in an over-the-top kind of way. "Let's make daisy chains with those younger children."

"Yes!" I said, trying my best to sound enthusiastic. "Let's!"

After that narrow escape we just had to stay out of the M&Ms way for the rest of the afternoon. It was a huge relief all round when school finally broke up. And it was even more of a relief when Fliss turned up at the next Brownie meeting with the form and her money. There was no going back now – assault course or not!

* * *

There were only two weeks between us handing in our forms and actually going away to camp. You can imagine how excited we were. We never seemed to talk about anything else.

"I can't wait!" laughed Kenny.

We were all sitting in her room a couple of days before the camp. "There'll be so many cool things to do! I've always wanted to have a bash at abseiling!"

"Yeah, 'having a bash' is probably right!" laughed Frankie. "Knowing you, you'll probably try to do it too fast and splat! – you'll be squashed on the wall."

Fliss sort of shivered.

"We're only joking Fliss," I reassured her. "It won't be like that – there'll be lots of fun stuff. It's going to be brilliant!"

"Do you think we ought to start practising for the Challenge?" Fliss asked.

We all stared at her with our mouths open.

"What, you mean you know?" asked Rosie.

"Yes," said Fliss slowly, as though we were all dummies. "And I really think we should practise so that the M&Ms don't beat us."

"Cool!" shouted Kenny. "Maybe we should go outside now and start climbing a few trees or something. What about press-ups, they're good."

I started to shake my head at Kenny, because I could see Fliss's shocked face.

"How will climbing trees help us to sing the best songs round the camp fire?" she asked.

Kenny looked blank. It wasn't often that she was speechless.

"It's something to do with opening your lungs properly." Frankie leapt to her rescue. "I've heard that you should exercise before you sing."

Rosie and I rolled our eyes at each other, and I tried not to giggle.

It was a relief when we were finally on the minibus heading for Foxton Glen. We knew that we couldn't keep the assault course a secret from Fliss for much longer, but we figured that we'd cope with it when it happened. Besides, we already had enough to worry about, dealing with the low-down behaviour of the M&Ms.

We'd all been lining up to get on the minibus, when they barged past us and nabbed the seats right in the middle. Alana Banana sat on the seat opposite them, which meant that we couldn't all sit together. So Kenny and Frankie sat in front of the Gruesome Twosome, Rosie and Fliss sat behind them and I sat in front of Alana Banana with – get this – Brown Owl. So we had an excellent journey to Foxton Glen – not! And it was all the fault of those selfish M&Ms. We were determined that they'd pay for it over the next few days.

"Here we are, girls!" Brown Owl called out, as we finally swung off the main road onto a twisty track. We all pressed our faces up to the windows so that we could see where we'd be staying for the next few days.

"Wow, isn't this cool!" yelled Kenny. "What's that over there?" She was pointing to something in the distance.

"That's the tower for the abseiling and the climbing wall," explained Brown Owl.

The minibus stopped.

"Right, can you please get off the minibus quickly and quietly," said Brown Owl, "and remember to collect all your bags."

We pushed and shoved our way off as quickly as we could. Apart from Fliss, who always has to check anywhere a million times to make sure she hasn't left anything behind.

We were all hyper, laughing and joking as we looked around – it was awesome. But we also realised that the dreaded moment had finally arrived.

"What are you so excited about?" Fliss asked, when she finally joined us.

Together, we pointed at the sign in front of us, which said, in huge letters: ASSAULT COURSE THIS WAY.

CHAPTER THREE

Poor Fliss! I've never seen anyone go as white so quickly. It was as though someone had sucked all the blood out of her face with a straw.

"Are you all right, Felicity?" Brown Owl asked anxiously.

But Fliss could only mumble and point to the sign.

"Assault course does sound a bit grim, doesn't it?" laughed Brown Owl. "But don't worry, because it's not going to be the assault course for much longer. I'll explain when the other Brownies get here."

Another minibus was driving towards us. When it stopped, the Brownies from 12th Cuddington spilled out. We recognised a few of them from school. We certainly recognised Regina Hill and Amanda Porter, who headed straight for the M&Ms and Alana 'Banana'. They stood in a silly little huddle screeching and chattering like chimps in a zoo.

As soon as they had settled down, Brown Owl explained what she had meant about the assault course. This camp was going to have the theme of children's TV programmes, so the assault course was going to be referred to as Blue Peter, the kitchen would be Grange Hill, and the toilet and shower blocks would be called Arnold and Doug!

There were twenty Brownies altogether, eleven from our pack and nine from the other. So there were going to be four tents of five, plus a tent for the grown-ups. The Sleepover Club were in a tent together and we didn't have to share with anyone else which was great. The M&Ms were sharing with Alana Palmer, the awful Amanda Porter and Regina Hill. Then there was a tent of Brownies from 12th Cuddington and another tent with girls from both packs, but it was OK because they all knew each other.

Brown Owl called each group a 'patrol' and we all had a name. We were Rugrats, the M&Ms and their group were Teletubbies, the group just from 12th were The Simpsons and the mixed group were Wombles. Pretty cool, huh? We really laughed when Brown Owl said that we had to call her Tom and the Brown Owl from 12th, Jerry!

A group of forest rangers had already started to put up our tents. Jerry said that three of them would be staying with us for the rest of the camp and we had to call them Paddington, Garfield and Scooby Doo!

I wondered how I would ever remember all those new names.

"Isn't this great?" I said to Rosie, as we took our stuff over to the tents.

"Yeah, but I don't think Fliss is very

happy," she replied. I looked across at Fliss. She looked really sulky and miserable.

"Right, Rugrats, this will be your tent," said Brown Owl. "This is Paddington and her ranger friends. You can help them finish putting up your tent, but you must do exactly as they say."

The rangers were really cool and fun. And actually I think they were quite pleased with us, because Kenny and I are used to putting up tents. We go camping a lot with our families, you see. We helped tighten the ropes and everything, while Frankie and Rosie tried to calm Fliss down. I just couldn't understand how anyone could get so freaked out over an assault course – especially one that was called Blue Peter. Still, Fliss does a lot of stuff that I don't understand.

When our tent was up we took our stuff inside. The tent itself was like a bell and had one big pole in the middle. We arranged our sleeping bags so that they fanned out like the spokes of a wheel. We would sleep with our heads in the middle by the pole, and our feet pointing out to the sides. It was a bit weird, but exciting, too.

I kind of like sleeping in a tent because it's all sort of squashed and cosy. But Fliss didn't like it at all. "There's just no room!" she kept wailing.

"Oh Fliss, shut up, will you!" snapped Kenny. "You knew it wasn't going to be The Savoy!"

Fliss's lip started to quiver a bit. The last thing we needed was any waterworks.

"Come on, Fliss, you'll get used to it!" I reassured her. "We're Rugrats, remember!"

"I wonder which Teletubbies the M&Ms are!" laughed Frankie.

"I don't know, but Amanda Porter definitely looks like one!" said Kenny and did and impression of her waddling along. We all laughed – even Fliss!

Brown Owl poked her head through the tent flap. "I'm glad to see that you're settling in," she said. "I expect you're all itching to get out and start doing things. So, go to

Arnold if you need to, then I'll meet you at Blue Peter in five minutes!"

"Great!" yelled Kenny.

She flew out of the tent, but the rest of us hung back. Fliss had started to do her impression of a quivering jelly again.

"I'm sure you won't have to go on the assault course if you don't want to," I told her.

"I'm rubbish at stuff like that, too," Rosie reassured her. "We'll go on it together. If we don't like it, we can always get off."

Fliss looked a bit brighter.

"And I'll stay with you, too," I told them. I quite like assault courses and things but I felt sorry for Fliss, and I thought that if Rosie really did want to have a proper go on it, I could look after Fliss.

"C'mon you lot. What's keeping you?" yelled Kenny. She rushed back into the tent all out of breath. You could tell that she was itching to go on the assault course.

"I'll go with action man here," said Frankie. "One of us had better keep an eye on her!" And she ran after Kenny.

The rest of us took our time. We went to the loos and when Fliss had played about in there as long as she possibly could, we made our way over to the assault course.

To be honest with you I didn't really know what to expect. I suppose I'd imagined scramble nets about six metres high and nothing but mud all around. But it wasn't like that at all. Actually it looked really pretty – there were big bushes on each side and it followed a sort of loop, so you could see where you started and finished but you couldn't see all the bits in between. It looked vast, but that was only because instead of there being one obstacle, there were two of the same kind next to each other. I guessed that that was so teams could compete against each other. Which reminded me about the Challenge on the last day.

"At last!" called Brown Owl when she saw us. "I thought Arnold must have swallowed you up!"

Two Brownies from The Simpsons ran past us. They were giggling together and looked as if they were having a great time. I couldn't wait to start.

"Fliss is a bit nervous about the assault— I mean, about Blue Peter," Rosie explained.

Fliss looked really annoyed with her.

"There's nothing to be worried about," Brown Owl reassured us. "Jerry and I are here to help you and the rangers are on the course, too. Just take your time and have fun."

"Come on, Fliss!" smiled Rosie. "We might as well have a go on it now we're here."

"Look, I'll go first, then you just follow me," I suggested.

Fliss nodded, so I set off. First you had to jump over a hurdle, then there was a ditch with a tree trunk over the top. The Brownies in front of me balanced on the trunk as though it was a tightrope. They moved along it really slowly so that they didn't fall into the mud underneath. I just copied what they did. It was great. I could hear Kenny and Frankie ahead of me, but I couldn't see them. I turned round. "Are you OK?" I shouted back.

Rosie gave me the thumbs-up sign and Fliss was actually laughing.

"You see," I called back. "There was nothing to worry about, was there?"

Once I knew that they were all right I just did my own thing. There were lots of things I'd seen people do on the television, like running through two rows of tyres, which was much more difficult than I'd thought it would be. But the hardest thing was getting over the top of the scramble nets and climbing down the other side. It took a while to get used to swaying about while you were climbing, but it was really exciting.

From the top of the nets, I could see the rest of the course. There was Emily Berryman slumped by the side of the underground crawl-through tunnel. She looked as though she was about to be sick. Amanda Porter was stuck in the swinging tyres and Kenny was pretending to be Tarzan on the rope swing. I climbed down the netting as fast as I could. I was desperate to have a go on the rest of the course.

I was just coming up to the underground tunnel when I heard screaming. It didn't register at first, but then I realised it was Fliss. I ran back and there she was – stuck at the top of the scramble nets.

"I can't move!" she cried. "I'm too scared."

Rosie was at the other side trying to coax her down. I climbed up to Fliss and tried to reassure her.

"You've done the worst part," I said. "All you've got to do now is reach over and pull yourself over to the other side."

"Easy for you to say!" Fliss squeaked.

I climbed up and showed her what to do, but it was no good, she just wouldn't move. When she'd been there for what seemed like hours I said, "There's Scooby Doo over there, talking to the M&Ms. I'll call her over, shall I?"

As soon as I said that, Fliss flung herself over the top of the nets and sort of slid down the other side. Rosie and I scrambled down after her. Fliss was lying in a heap at the bottom.

"I told you I hated assault courses!" she sobbed.

"Don't worry, you won't have to go on it again," I told her.

Me and my big mouth!

When Fliss had recovered enough, we all walked round to the end of the assault course, where everyone else had gathered.

"Have a little problem, did you?" Emma Hughes asked Fliss cattily.

Fliss blushed.

"Had a few little problems yourselves!" retorted Kenny, looking from Emily Berryman to Amanda Porter. Then it was their turn to look embarrassed.

"We'll still beat you bunch of losers in the Blue Peter Challenge!" said Emma Hughes angrily.

"Blue Peter Challenge?" whimpered Fliss, as the truth suddenly hit her. "You mean the Challenge is over the assault course?"

Kenny ignored Fliss and faced the M&Ms full on. "There's absolutely no way you're going to beat us!" spat Kenny. "And that's a promise!"

The rest of us looked at each other. When Kenny wants something badly enough, the rest of us have to suffer for it. But we didn't know then just how badly Kenny wanted to beat the M&Ms.

CHAPTER FOUR

After we'd all had a go on the assault course, Brown Owl took us to look round some of the other activities we'd be doing at Foxton Glen. Kenny was still mad at the M&Ms. I thought she'd never get over it. She didn't even perk up when we walked over to the climbing wall and the abseiling tower.

"What's up with her?" I mouthed to Frankie. But she just shrugged her shoulders.

And Fliss wasn't a bundle of laughs, either. She was still all twitchy about the assault course and kept saying there was no

way that she was ever going on it again,
Challenge or not. That of course just made
Kenny madder still.

It didn't help that Emma Hughes and her
stupid friends kept whispering together,
then looking over at us and giggling.

"They're really getting on my nerves!"
said Rosie.

"You and me both," I replied.

We were all a bit on edge because we were
expecting Kenny to have a go at them at any
moment. But luckily she didn't. She just kept
giving them evil looks.

We were walking back towards our tents
when Rosie pointed to something and asked
Brown Owl what it was.

"That's one of the nature ponds," Brown
Owl explained. "There are a few frogs and
things in it, so we can look at the creatures
in their natural habitat."

"They won't get into our tents, will they?"
asked Fliss anxiously.

"No, Felicity, they won't hop that far!"
laughed Brown Owl. "And we won't be

eating frogs' legs for supper either. But we will be eating pasta and Teletubbies are on kitchen duty, The Simpsons will be waitresses and Rugrats are going to be our orderlies. Wombles, you can be on litter patrol – you should be good at that!"

We all laughed.

"So, Emma," Brown Owl continued, "when we get back to the tents could you and your patrol get yourselves ready for a bit of action in the kitchen. The rest of you will be playing games with Jerry and the rangers until supper."

Kenny had been very quiet while we were out, but when we got back to our tent she started leaping about.

"Looks like the old Kenny's made a comeback!" laughed Frankie.

"I've got a plan. It's totally brilliant and it's going to finish off the M&Ms once and for all!" she told us.

"Well go on then – spill!" I commanded.

"No way! I'm going to keep this one quiet. But you'll hear about it soon enough!" she said, grinning from ear to ear. "All I want you to do is cover up for me if anyone notices I'm missing."

"Charming!" said Fliss. "You won't tell us what you're going to do but you want us to cover for you. That doesn't sound very fair!"

The rest of us rolled our eyes. Fliss is very big on things 'being fair'.

"Just do it, OK!" commanded Kenny in a tone of voice which told us that we shouldn't mess with her plans.

In our bags we'd all brought enough goodies for three midnight feasts. Kenny had brought hers in a large ice-cream carton. She went over to her bag, took it out, and tipped everything in it onto her sleeping bag. Mini Mars bars, jelly babies, lollipops and Black Jacks spilled everywhere. She scooped them back into her bag and skipped out of the tent with the ice-cream carton.

"What on earth is she going to do?" asked Frankie, staring after her.

"You know what she's like," said Fliss.

46

"Do you think we should follow her to make sure she's not doing anything stupid."

"She'd kill us if she spotted us," said Rosie.

"We'll just have to do as she says and cover for her," I said. "I can hear the others outside. Come on, let's go and play some games!"

We ran outside and joined The Simpsons, Wombles and the rangers. Then we had a cool time playing an enormous game of Cops and Robbers. When someone asked where Kenny was, we just said that she had a stomach ache and was lying down. But then of course Jerry thought she ought to go and check on her, so I had to think fast.

Unfortunately, tripping up and gashing open my knee was the only thing I could think of. And very painful it was, too – I hope Kenny appreciated it. Still, it kept Jerry occupied and stopped her worrying about Kenny.

When Tom called us all for supper, Fliss looked really panicked. "What if they go to fetch Kenny and find she's not there!"

she said.

But just then, as if she was a mind-reader, Kenny appeared. She strolled out of our tent with a humungous grin on her face, and muddy marks on her trousers.

"Are you feeling better now?" asked Jerry. "Do you think you might be able to manage a little supper?"

"You bet, I'm starving!" Kenny replied.

"B– but what about your stomach ache?" squeaked Rosie.

"I haven't got one," Kenny looked puzzled, then she cottoned on. "I mean, it's gone now," she said.

"The lie-down must have done you good," said Jerry.

Kenny just smiled.

We all went to sit down and The Simpsons brought us our food.

"Mmm, this isn't half bad!" said Kenny, slurping down her pasta like a pig.

We all looked at her really suspiciously. The M&Ms had cooked it and she never praises anything that they're involved in.

"You haven't sabotaged it, have you?" asked Frankie suspiciously.

"Get real!" laughed Kenny. "I'm hardly likely to ruin the food we've all got to eat now, am I?"

"So what have you been doing?" I asked.

But Kenny just shook her head and kept tapping the side of her nose. "You'll find out soon enough," she told us.

When everyone had finished eating, we got up to collect the plates.

"Nice meal!" Kenny whispered to Emma Hughes, as she took her plate.

The M&Ms looked at Kenny suspiciously, but she just smiled and took the plates into Grange Hill.

After pudding we had to wash up, which didn't sound like much fun. I hate washing up at home, but then I'm not in the middle of a field acting stupid with my friends, am I? We had a real laugh – though we seemed to wash more of each other than the plates! I noticed that Kenny was already kind of wet, but she wouldn't say why.

By the time we'd finished, we were all soaking. And kind of tired. Have you noticed how when you're at home you just want to stay up late, but the first night you're away you want to go to bed early, just because it's all new?

It seemed like everyone felt the same because we were all yawning as we sat outside singing. I'd assumed that there'd be a camp fire every evening, but there wasn't one that first night, which was really disappointing. Brown Owl said it was because they take a long time to prepare, but she promised we'd have one on the other nights.

It was nearly dark as we all trooped back to our tents to collect our toilet bags. As soon as we got there, Kenny grabbed her ice-cream carton and peeped out of the tent flap.

"What are you looking for?" Frankie whispered.

"The M&Ms," Kenny replied. "Ssh, they're coming!"

She hurried back inside and waited for them to walk past. She was holding tightly to the carton she was holding. There seemed to be a lot of water sloshing about in it.

"Right, you lot go to Doug and delay the Gruesome Twosome and their mates as long as you can. Understood?" commanded Kenny.

"Yes, Sir!" Frankie, Rosie and I saluted her together. Fliss just looked cross.

"I wonder what she's got planned," said Rosie as we walked to the shower block.

"Dunno," shrugged Frankie, "but it certainly looks like it's something big!"

"I don't see why she couldn't let us in on it, though," moaned Fliss.

"She must have her reasons," said Frankie. "Anyway, remember, we've got to delay the M&Ms as long as possible."

We all went into the shower block. The girls from The Simpsons patrol were just leaving. They smiled and said "Goodnight".

"They're really friendly, aren't they?" said Fliss.

"Unlike some people," said Rosie, scowling at the M&Ms.

"Where's your horrible little friend?" asked Emma Hughes.

"Kenny? She's got a stomach ache," replied Frankie.

"Something serious I hope," smiled Amanda Porter.

The rest of her group laughed their stupid little laughs.

"It must have been something you cooked," said Fliss, who was hovering in the doorway.

"Well you certainly didn't eat much," Emma Hughes snapped. "I would have thought a wimp like you should be building up your strength. You're going to look a complete wally when you get on the assault course again."

Fliss went bright red. But so did Emily Berryman and she started to walk towards the door.

I think we all panicked a bit then. Fliss more than the rest of us. As she was in the doorway, it was up to Fliss to stop Emily Berryman as she went past. And Fliss definitely wasn't up to giving her a rugby tackle. She started dithering, dropped her toilet bag and stooped to pick it up. Berryman didn't notice and tripped over her. Then all the stuff from her toilet bag spilt all over the floor and she ended up falling on top of it. It was like something out of a cartoon, but we couldn't have planned it better if we'd tried.

We all bent down to help pick everything up. And of course Frankie, Rosie and I kept picking up Emily Berryman's things sort of accidentally-on-purpose. So it took quite a while to get everything sorted out.

"You're so clumsy!" snarled Emma Hughes to Fliss as they were leaving.

"So is *she*," Rosie said, looking at Emily Berryman. "And we wouldn't want Fliss to be contaminated with any of the germs from her things."

The M&Ms and their cronies flounced out, and we all cracked up.

53

"What about Kenny?" wailed Fliss. "What if she hasn't finished yet?"

"Oh, but I have!" said Kenny suddenly appearing. "I've just been hiding behind a bush watching you all. Nice one, Fliss!"

Kenny still wouldn't tell us what she had done. She just had this big I'm-so-clever grin on her face and kept saying, "You'll find out soon enough!"

We all finished washing and brushing our teeth, then went back to our tent to get ready for bed. We did our striptease in our sleeping bags, then sat in a circle round the pole in the middle.

"Let's have our midnight feast now!" I said. "I'm so tired, I don't think I can keep awake much longer!"

The others laughed. I'm always the first one of us to fall asleep.

We emptied all our sweets onto Kenny's sleeping bag. Her ones looked a bit gross because they'd been loose in the bottom of her bag and were covered in all sorts of bits of fluff.

"How do we decide what we're going to eat for our midnight feast tonight and what we're going to save?" asked Rosie.

"You mean, how are we going to stop ourselves from eating everything in one go?" laughed Frankie.

"And how do we stop the swamp monster breaking in and stealing all our sweets?" said Kenny in a really spooky voice.

"Don't!" squealed Fliss.

"I'm not scaring you, am I?" asked Kenny, in the same spooky voice.

Before Fliss could answer, a loud piercing scream seemed to rip through the campsite. We all clung together, hardly daring to breathe.

CHAPTER FIVE

"What was that?" squeaked Frankie.

"I don't know, but it came from the tent next door," said Rosie.

We all looked at each other.

"The M&Ms!" we said together.

"It sounds as though Brown Owl's in there now," said Fliss.

We all went to the tent flap and peered out. We could hear someone wailing and we were pretty sure that it was Emma Hughes. Then we heard Brown Owl.

"I'm sure it's just a freak thing, Emma," she was saying. "Why on earth would anyone

56

want to put a frog in your sleeping bag?"

Well, we just collapsed in a heap when we heard that.

"A frog!" squealed Frankie to Kenny. "You actually put a frog in her sleeping bag!"

Kenny was nodding and spluttering.

"Sssh! Brown Owl's coming!" said Fliss.

We all dived into our sleeping bags.

"Are you all right in here, girls?" asked Brown Owl.

"What was that noise?" asked Fliss in her weakest little voice.

"Oh, nothing to worry about," said Brown Owl. "You haven't been into the Teletubbies tent for anything, have you?"

"Oh no, we wouldn't do that!" said Kenny.

"Hmm," said Brown Owl thoughtfully. "I don't want there to be any trouble. I want this to be a happy camp."

"Oh, but it is!" gushed Rosie. "We're having a great time, aren't we?"

"Yes!" we all spluttered, trying not to laugh.

"That's good!" said Brown Owl. "You're

cooking tomorrow, so you'll have to be up by seven. I'd try to get some sleep if I were you! Sweet dreams!"

When we were sure that Brown Owl had gone, we all turned on our torches and sat up.

"That was wicked!" I squealed.

"I just hope the M&Ms don't suss out who it was and do it back to us, though," shuddered Fliss. "I'd die if I found a frog in my sleeping bag."

"We'll have to try not to leave our tent for too long tomorrow, just in case," said Frankie seriously. "And we'd better make sure that the flap is tightly shut tonight."

Kenny and I got up and fastened it as securely as we could. Not even King Kong would have been able to get through when we'd finished with it!

"Anyway, we should be celebrating getting one over the M&Ms!" said Kenny. "Chocolate frog anyone?"

We collapsed in giggles again.

Our midnight feast goodies were still scattered over Kenny's sleeping bag. We scooped them all together again and roughly divided them into three piles. We put what we weren't going to eat that night into two plastic bags and left them by the tent pole.

I ate what felt like my weight in chocolate and declared, "I'm stuffed now!"

"Me too!" agreed Rosie.

"I guess we ought to try to sleep if we've got to be up early tomorrow," suggested Frankie.

I expected Kenny to disagree, but she was already snuggling down in her sleeping bag. "Seven o'clock!" she grumbled. "What sort of crazy time is that?"

It felt strange to be having a sleepover in a tent. Especially as we were all suddenly too tired to sing our sleepover song. But at least we had another two 'under canvas' sleepovers to look forward to.

Are you all right there, I'm not walking too fast, am I? The playground isn't too far away now, then we can have a go on the swings. I bet Kenny will be a lot livelier today than she was on that first morning at camp. Boy is she grumpy when she gets up. Especially when Brown Owl has woken her up at the crack of dawn!

"Tell her to shut up!" moaned Kenny, pulling a pillow over her head.

The rest of us dragged ourselves out of our sleeping bags and wandered around bleary-eyed. But by the time we'd got ourselves dressed, and dressed Kenny because she said she was too tired to do it herself, we were ready for anything. Well, almost anything, we weren't ready for the M&Ms, that's for sure.

As soon as we saw them, we knew we were in trouble.

"We'll get you for that!" hissed Emma Hughes, as we dished out baked beans and toast.

"I don't know what you're talking about!" Kenny said innocently.

"You'll be sorry, that's all!" said Emily

Berryman, snatching her plate from me.

"What do you think they'll do?" whispered Fliss. "I hope they haven't been into our tent while we've been cooking breakfast."

We rushed back to the tent as soon as we could, but nothing seemed to be missing. We felt inside our sleeping bags, too, but there were no frogs in any of them.

"We can't stay in the tent all day!" said Fliss.

"We won't have to, all the patrols are doing different activities, so we'll be spread out across the site," explained Frankie. "And we'll be back at the campsite together for lunch, so if the M&Ms go anywhere near our tent we'll know about it."

"I suppose we'll just have to hope that their group doesn't get back before us, won't we?" said Rosie.

We didn't have the chance to worry about that for long; we soon became busy trying to encourage Fliss down the abseiling tower. I mean it wasn't really high or anything, Fliss was just in scaredy-cat mode. It's crazy. You know that she can do something, but she doesn't think she can and wimps out.

Paddington came abseiling with us, as well as another cool instructor from Foxton Glen called Danny. Whenever he called Fliss forward, she'd go to the top of the tower, take one look down and go all feeble. I felt a bit sorry for her, especially as Kenny kept having a go at her.

"Fliss don't be such a baby!" she yelled. "Look at all the ropes round you! It's absolutely impossible for you to fall, isn't it, Danny?"

"Sure is!" said Danny. "I'm holding tight onto you up here!"

He winked at Paddington, who blushed big time.

I thought Fliss was going to be up there all day. We tried encouraging her. Kenny tried threatening her. We even tried bribing her with new nail varnish, but nothing worked.

Then she saw the M&Ms. They'd been doing some archery and were heading back to the campsite for lunch. Amanda Porter suddenly turned to look at us and saw Fliss hovering about at the top of the tower. She said something to the M&Ms and they both turned round. Then they started to walk towards us.

I could see Fliss getting more and more panicky. She looked as though she was going to topple off the tower in fright. Especially when the awful witches started to cluck like chickens and flap their arms about. But that kind of spurred her on.

"Right, I'm going down now," Fliss suddenly told Danny.

She turned round and started to abseil down the tower slowly. We all yelled and shouted encouragement. When she got to the bottom, Fliss sort of wobbled about while Paddington removed her harness.

"That was cool!" laughed Kenny. "Now we know how to get you to do stuff – we'll just ask the M&Ms to come and make fun of you!"

The Gruesome Twosome and their

cronies were already walking back towards our tents. I was so glad that Fliss had proved them wrong. But that's Fliss – she can always produce a surprise when you're least expecting it!

When we got back to the campsite we had to make sandwiches for everyone's lunch, which was a bit of a drag. But the other patrols had to collect wood for the camp fire, which sounded even more of a pain. Our patrol was going to help Brown Owl actually build the fire later in the afternoon. I couldn't wait.

While we were making the sandwiches, we took it in turns to keep popping back to check on the tent. Until Brown Owl became suspicious. But by then all the others were hanging round waiting for their lunch anyway.

"I bet the M&Ms are too scared to break into our tent," said Kenny confidently. "One-nil to us!"

"Let's hope it stays that way!" said Frankie grimly.

After lunch we had just the best time canoeing. We had to concentrate so hard on what the instructor told us that we didn't have a moment to even think about the M&Ms. By the time we got back to our tent, I was exhausted. And then we had to go and get everything ready for dinner round the camp fire. It's hard work being a Brownie sometimes!

It was pretty cool helping Brown Owl build the fire. It's a lot more difficult to light than it looks and it seemed to take ages before we even saw any smoke. Then gradually it built up and the flames got quite fierce. It could have been kind of dangerous, I guess, but we were all given a talk about not getting too close and not acting stupid around it. Even Kenny took notice of that. And we also had a fire drill with pretend buckets of water, so that if it did get out of hand we'd all know what to do.

For supper we were having jacket potatoes wrapped in foil and baked in the fire. They were going to take quite a long time to cook, so while we were waiting Brown Owl asked each patrol to go off on their own and come up with a song, dance or poem they could perform in front of the others the following evening.

Kenny did her I-told-you-so face and Fliss looked really excited. I think she was all set to start practising one of our dance routines straight away, but Kenny was having none of that. "OK, let's start training for the Blue Peter Challenge!" she said.

Fliss went white. "B– but I'm not going on the assault course again," she stuttered.

"Look, Fliss, if you can master the abseiling wall, the assault course will be a doddle," Kenny reassured her. "Just imagine the M&Ms are laughing at you!"

"Thanks a lot!" said Fliss crossly. "Anyway, we're supposed to be working on our performance for tomorrow night!"

"Don't be so wet!" said Kenny. "We're always doing silly dances at our sleepovers, we know loads of routines really well already. But we haven't done any practice for the Challenge. Let's all sprint down to our tent, do ten sit-ups, sprint back and do some press-ups!"

We knew by the tone of her voice that she was deadly serious.

"Come on! We want to win this thing, don't we?" she yelled and hared off.

The rest of us ran after her, gasping and wheezing. We were totally exhausted by the time Brown Owl called us for supper. It was as if we were in the army, the way Kenny was putting us through our paces. It was a real relief to sit down and eat our baked potatoes!

Fortunately we weren't sitting near the M&Ms, so they didn't put us off our food. But I don't think anything would have put me off the marshmallows we toasted over the fire for pudding. They were yummy!

After we'd eaten, we all sang songs round the fire which was well cool! We sang 'Camp Fire's Burning' in rounds, 'Do Your Ears Hang Low?' with all the actions and we finished off with 'Taps' – which is what we always sing at the end of Brownie meetings.

Tired, but happy, we all staggered back to our tents. We were almost there when Kenny stopped us. "Sssh!" she hissed. "There's someone in our tent!"

CHAPTER SIX

We stopped in our tracks and listened. Kenny was right, there was certainly somebody rustling about inside our tent. It just had to be those M&Ms.

"Right, I'm going to get them for this!" whispered Kenny.

She started to tie up the tent flap.

"Don't let them get out whatever you do," she warned. "And try not to let them know you're here."

She ran off towards Grange Hill. We didn't know what she had in mind. We were too busy worrying about what we'd do if the

M&Ms tried to get out.

Kenny was back in a flash. She was carrying a huge tube of squirty cream.

"You haven't stolen that, have you?" Fliss looked shocked.

"'Course not," Kenny replied. "I've just borrowed it."

She bent down and quietly began to undo the tent flap. Then we all crouched on the ground, so that when the M&Ms appeared we would be ready for them.

"I think they're coming out!" hissed Rosie.

We all stood up. My heart was beating like crazy. When the tent flap opened we all started screaming and Kenny sprayed cream like a demon. It was only when this tall blob started squealing and stumbling into us that we realised it wasn't the M&Ms at all. It was Snowy Owl – Fliss's Auntie Jill!

"What on earth is going on here?" asked Brown Owl who had come across because of all the noise we were making.

"We thought that someone had broken into our tent," explained Kenny sheepishly.

"Well as you can see, no one has," said Brown Owl. "Fliss's mum sent her some clean underwear and Snowy Owl was putting it in your tent."

Brown Owl looked furious, but fortunately Snowy Owl was laughing. "I finished my course this afternoon," she explained, "so I came down to join the camp. I thought I'd surprise you, Felicity, as I haven't seen you for such a long time! But I guess I should have just given you your underwear, rather than sneaking into your tent."

Fliss was as red as a beetroot. I think it was because everyone had heard about her mum sending down some clean underwear. She was more embarrassed about that than the fact that we'd covered her Auntie Jill with cream.

All the other Brownies had gathered round us. Unfortunately the M&Ms were right at the front, sneering at us, which was just awful.

"At least there's one good thing," said

Frankie when Brown Owl had sent everyone away and we were cleaning up the mess.

"Oh yeah, what would that be then?" asked Kenny.

"The M&Ms haven't managed to sabotage us today," said Frankie gleefully. "I bet they couldn't think of a way to get back at us. They're just not bright enough. Shame, isn't it?"

We all laughed.

We were ready to go to the shower block with our toilet bags when Kenny said, "Let's sprint to the showers, do push-ups against the wall, shower and stuff, and then jog back!"

Now I like Kenny as much as anyone, but this was getting a bit out of hand. It really was like being in the army. Besides, we were all totally exhausted.

"Get real, Kenny!" moaned Frankie. "This camp is supposed to be fun."

"But we've got to win the Challenge!" said Kenny. It was like it was the only thing that mattered to her.

"I've already told you I'm not going on the assault course again," Fliss said. "And I'm going to tell Auntie Jill that I'm not tomorrow. She won't make me do anything I don't want to."

Kenny screwed up her eyes and looked at us all in a fury. "Well I'm going to beat the M&Ms, even if you're all going to wimp out." She spat out the words and sprinted off towards the showers.

We all looked at each other, then trotted after her.

Fortunately, it was quiet when we got there. I think the other Brownies must have washed while we were apologising to Snowy Owl and cleaning everything up. It had taken ages to wash all the cream off the tent. Some had even got onto Rosie's sleeping bag.

We were a bit sticky with cream ourselves, so we all decided to have a shower. There was a cubicle for each of us, but unfortunately there wasn't any hot water left. We were all absolutely freezing by the time we'd got out and dried ourselves.

"Well at least that's cooled us down!" laughed Rosie. "Maybe we should jog back to our tent after all – just to warm up a bit!"

So after brushing our teeth, that's what we did. We laughed and giggled all the way back, which sort of broke the tension a bit, because we were still feeling a bit annoyed with Kenny. She was so obsessed by the whole Blue Peter Challenge that she was starting to spoil the camp for the rest of us.

When we got back we could hear the M&Ms in the tent next door. They were obviously having a midnight feast, although it was nowhere near midnight yet.

"Aren't these Choc Dips just scrummy!" Emma Hughes was saying.

"Mmm, they can't be as gorgeous as these milk bottles!" said Emily Berryman in her gruff voice. We sometimes call her 'the Goblin' because of her deep voice – and because she's so small.

The other Teletubbies were all cooing over their sweets too.

"You'd think no one else had ever had a

midnight feast before!" grumbled Kenny. "They're just so pathetic."

She started to howl like a wolf and the rest of us joined in.

"Oh grow up!" shouted Emily Berryman. "We know it's you, Laura McKenzie. Couldn't you think of anything more original?"

Kenny looked furious. But before she could say anything Emma Hughes piped up, "Is Felicity there?"

Fliss pulled a face then said, "Yes, what do you want?"

"Hadn't you better go and put on that underwear your mummy sent?" Emma Hughes asked in a sickly voice. "You dirtied your other knickers at the top of the abseiling tower, didn't you? You're a big baby, Felicity DirtyBottom!"

We couldn't see Fliss's face because it was kind of dark, but I could tell that she was blushing by the heat that was coming off her! She hates people making fun of her, and she's especially prickly about her surname – it's Sidebotham, but nobody ever says it like that!

Amanda Porter joined in taunting poor Fliss. "You'll need even more clean underwear when we've wiped the floor with you in the Blue Peter Challenge!" she smarmed in her silly fat voice. "You all will!"

"Come on!" Kenny said through her teeth. "We're not going to listen to these idiots. They're all talk – no action!"

We scrambled back into our tent. Nobody spoke. We got undressed and ready for bed in complete silence, for just about the first time ever!

After what seemed like ages Kenny said quietly, "Now do you see why we've got to train hard to beat them?"

We all nodded. Except Fliss. "I'm still going to tell Auntie Jill that I don't want to take part in the Challenge," she mumbled.

Before Kenny could have another go at her, Frankie leapt in. "Well, we'll all need our strength, won't we?" she laughed. "What about a few munchies before bedtime? If those stupid M&Ms can make such a lot of noise when they eat their midnight feast, we can make twice as much when we eat ours!"

"Yes!" we all shouted at the tops of our voices.

We all scrambled about around the tent pole, but before we could find the sweets we'd saved for that night's feast a torch flashed through the tent flap. We all jumped, but it was only Brown Owl.

"I don't know what's going on between you and Emma and her friends," she said firmly. "But whatever it is, I want it to stop."

"It's not just us—" Rosie started to protest.

"I know and I don't want to hear any more," said Brown Owl. "I've spoken to the girls next door and they promised me that whatever petty squabbles you've had in the past are over. I hope you can say the same thing."

We could feel her staring at us all, although we didn't dare look her in the face.

"Well?"

"Yes, everything's fine now," mumbled

Frankie. "There won't be any more trouble."

We all nodded our heads reluctantly.

"I'm very pleased to hear it," Brown Owl smiled. "So get some sleep, because you've another busy day tomorrow. Breakfast round the camp fire first thing! Sleep well!"

Kenny and I fastened the tent flap behind her, then we turned to the others.

"What do you reckon to that?" said Rosie.

"Well, I guess if that's what the M&Ms said – and meant it – we'll just have to play it cool with them until camp's finished," I said.

"But what about the Challenge?" asked Kenny.

"We'll have to abandon it!" said Fliss sounding livelier than she had done for days.

"I don't know about that," said Frankie quickly. She knew that Kenny wouldn't give in so easily. "I think we should have our midnight feast and sleep on it!"

We all looked around the tent again and rummaged about in our bags. But none of us could find any sweets.

"OK, this isn't funny!" Kenny sounded

very agitated. "Who's got the grub? One of you must have taken it from the tent pole."

We all shook our heads, then we looked in our bags again. And in our sleeping bags, our toilet bags and our wellingtons. Nothing!

"You don't think Snowy Owl took it, do you?" asked Rosie. "She was in here, wasn't she?"

"Don't be crazy, she wouldn't do that!" said Fliss indignantly. "I reckon it's the M&Ms. They must've been eating our midnight feast!"

Just then we heard lots of giggling outside our tent.

"That's right, Knicker Girl!" screeched Emma Hughes. "And very scrummy it was, too!"

"OK, that's it!" screamed Kenny. "This means war!"

And by the look in her eyes, we knew that she meant it.

CHAPTER SEVEN

I don't think any of us slept well that night. It's just not the same having a sleepover without a midnight feast! And I guess the rest of us were worried about what kind of revenge Kenny was planning for the M&Ms. She definitely had something in mind, because she kept mumbling about it in her sleep.

"Splat Goblin's face," she murmured. "Kick Hughes water."

None of it made sense of course, and in the morning Kenny denied saying anything at all. But she was still determined to get back at the M&Ms. Big time!

"We've got one more day to get ourselves in shape for the Assault Course Challenge!" she told us as soon as we woke up. "So we're going to train for it in every spare minute we have."

The rest of us groaned. Fliss pursed up her lips but didn't say anything.

"Teletubbies are on cooking duty, aren't they?" said Rosie.

"I think so, why?" asked Frankie.

"I was just thinking that we could raid their tent and try to get our midnight feast back while they're busy," replied Rosie.

"We could do," said Kenny, "but I'm starving. Let's go for breakfast first, or I'll waste away!"

We got dressed as fast as we could and ran to the toilet block. Everybody else must have had the same idea because there was a massive queue.

"Oh man!" moaned Kenny, jiggling about. "I'm going to wet myself if we have to wait much longer."

"You should all start wearing nappies!" smirked Emma Hughes, who was just emerging from Arnold. "We've always known that you were babies!"

Frankie and I had to use all our strength to stop Kenny from swinging for her. But even by the time we'd got to the front of the queue, Kenny was still seething. "Stupid witches!" she was mumbling. "I'm going to get them!"

Fliss, in contrast, hadn't said anything. In fact she'd hardly spoken since we got up. She kept looking round as though she was searching for someone. As soon as we got to the camp fire and she saw Snowy Owl, she sprinted over to her.

"Looks like she's going to get out of the Blue Peter Challenge," Rosie whispered to me. But I wasn't so sure. Fliss wasn't looking too happy. We left Frankie to try to calm Kenny down, snatched some toast from Emily Berryman in Grange Hill and wandered over to Snowy Owl.

"But I'm terrified of going on the assault

course, Auntie Jill!" Fliss was moaning. "And I'm no good at it anyway."

"That's a ridiculous attitude, Felicity," said Snowy Owl sternly. "You don't know what you're capable of until you try it."

We quietly went to sit down beside Fliss.

"That's what being a Guide is all about," continued Snowy Owl. "It's about gaining confidence in things and learning some independence."

"Fliss, don't worry about the Challenge," I said. "We'll help you."

Rosie nodded and squeezed Fliss's arm.

Snowy Owl smiled at us. "And it's about working as a team," she said. "You can only try your best, Fliss, that's all anybody asks of you. Right, girls, I'll leave you to it."

She left us looking into the fire, not really knowing what to say to Fliss.

"She's changed," said Fliss slowly. "Just because that course she went on from work used an assault course as a 'team building exercise' she thinks everybody should go on one!"

Poor Fliss, her aunt had suddenly gone all assertive on her, and her chance of getting out of the Challenge had gone.

"Look Fliss, try to look at this in a positive way," said Rosie soothingly. "You're as sporty as any of us. You can easily manage the assault course, it's just a case of believing in yourself."

"Yeah," I agreed. "So instead of looking at the scramble net and thinking, I'm going to get stuck at the top of that, you've got to think, it's just like climbing up a wobbly fence and that's easy!"

Fliss looked at us and smiled a watery kind of smile. "I guess so!" she mumbled.

Before we had time to reassure her some more, Kenny came flying towards us. "Operation Sweety Rescue is on for lunchtime!" she said. "We're going to raid the M&Ms tent while they make lunch."

It sounded fun, but I wasn't so sure it was going to be that easy.

Before lunch our patrol had a go at archery. It was well cool. And Fliss was good at it, which boosted her confidence no end. In fact she became quite a pain, reminding us how much better she was at archery than the rest of us.

"It's a pity there's no archery in the Challenge then, isn't it?" said Kenny sharply.

That soon shut Fliss up.

Kenny was still way too obsessed with the Challenge. At lunchtime, as we were walking back to the campsite, she even told us all what our weaknesses were.

"You don't take it seriously enough," she told Frankie. "And Lyndz, you don't put enough effort into it. Rosie, you're always looking round to see what everybody else is doing, and Fliss, well you're just a wimp, aren't you?"

That was really the last straw. We were all sick of Kenny telling us that we should be training all the time. I mean this wasn't the Olympics, was it? It wasn't even Gladiators. It was just some end-of-camp competition, which was supposed to be a bit of a laugh.

"If that's your attitude, Kenny, maybe we

shouldn't compete at all," said Frankie angrily. "I'm sure you're more than capable of beating everyone else single-handed."

It was really weird hearing Frankie speak to Kenny like that. They've been best friends like forever. But I guess that's why she could say what the rest of us were only thinking.

Back at the campsite Frankie headed straight for our tent. The rest of us followed her, but Kenny slunk off on her own.

"I'm sick of her going on like that," Frankie told us. "She's spoiling everything."

"Imagine how *I* feel!" said Fliss. "She's always calling me a wimp and putting me down."

"I know, and it's not fair," Rosie reassured her.

I looked out of the tent flap and I could see Kenny just sort of mooching around by herself. I felt kind of sorry for her. She was only trying to get one over the M&Ms and the rest of us wanted to do that, too. It's just that sometimes Kenny gets too carried away. I left the others to their complaining and went to see if she was all right.

"Hiya, Lyndz," she said kind of sheepishly when she saw me. "Is everything OK?"

"Pretty much," I told her. "But I think you've upset everybody."

Kenny just shrugged. Then she brightened up. "Maybe they'll forgive me if I get our midnight feast back from the Gruesome Twosome's tent," she said excitedly. "Will you help me?"

I wasn't so sure. I mean it's all right when all five of us do something like that together, but what would happen if just the two of us got caught?

"Come on, Lyndz, please," Kenny pleaded. "The M&Ms are preparing lunch, I've just checked. It won't take a minute."

Kenny was already undoing the flap of the M&Ms tent. Well I couldn't let her do it all by herself, could I? I went and joined her.

"I'll stay here," I whispered, "to keep a lookout!"

"It'll take too long for me to look through their stuff by myself," Kenny whispered back. "You'll have to come in, too, and we'll keep checking to make sure that no one's coming."

Very reluctantly, I crept inside.

Although the M&Ms were sleeping in the same kind of tent as us, it looked completely different. In our tent there was stuff all over the place, whereas in theirs everything was in neat piles at the bottom of each sleeping bag. It had this nasty smell of very stinky socks, too.

I didn't really like rummaging about in other people's things, but I told myself that they'd done it to us

"I can't find anything. What about you?" I asked Kenny. "You don't suppose they ate everything, do you? Or maybe they took the sweets with them, just in case we did this."

"Nah," replied Kenny confidently. "I saw them leave and they certainly didn't have anything with them. And not even that fatty Amanda Porter could have eaten all our sweets in one sitting."

We rummaged about some more, but it was hopeless.

"I'm going to kill them for this!" hissed Kenny.

Then a voice outside asked, "Kenny? Lyndz? Is that you?"

My heart nearly jumped out of my mouth.

"It's me, Frankie." She popped her head through the flap. "I think lunch is ready and I reckon the M&Ms could be back at any minute. You'd better hurry up!"

"Come on, let's go!" I said to Kenny. I grabbed her by her sleeve and she stumbled and fell – right into the line of wellies neatly arranged at the edge of the tent. As they all toppled over like dominoes, sweets began to spill out.

"Oooh, gross!" squealed Kenny. "They've been hiding our sweets in their boots!"

"Never mind that now!" I screeched. "Come on!"

We grabbed the bags of sweets and flew out of the tent. Frankie pushed us into our own tent just as Brown Owl was coming round the corner.

"Lunch is ready, girls!" she said, popping

her head through the flap. "Didn't you hear me calling?"

"Sorry, we've just been talking about how much we're enjoying ourselves here," gushed Rosie.

"Well that's great, but we're toasting sandwiches round the fire and we really all need to be together for that," said Brown Owl.

"We'll be right there!" said Frankie.

We waited until we were sure Brown Owl had gone, then we all collapsed into giggles. Kenny and I tossed the bags of sweets onto the floor of the tent to show the others. Then we shoved them right to the bottom of her sleeping bag – no one would dare to look for anything in there!

"Our sweets have probably been contaminated by those stinky M&Ms," Kenny said, pulling a face.

"At least we've got them back," said Frankie. "Thanks, you two."

"That's OK," said Kenny.

I raised my eyes to her. "And…" I

prompted.

Kenny looked puzzled.

"You're sorry…" I continued.

"Oh yes. I'm sorry I was awful about you competing in the Assault Course Challenge!" she said in a huge rush.

"We can only try our best," said Frankie. "You must remember that, Kenny."

Kenny nodded. "I'll try," she said sheepishly. Then she brightened up. "I've got a new recruit for our team, too," she told us, grinning from ear to ear.

"Who?" we all asked together.

Kenny wriggled about a bit and pulled something from underneath her jumper. It was a teddy bear. "I've kidnapped him from the M&Ms tent," she told us smugly. "And if they want to see this bear alive again, they're going to have to show us a bit of respect!"

CHAPTER EIGHT

Before we could ask Kenny what she was planning on doing with the bear, she leapt up and said, "Come on, let's go for lunch. I'm starving."

Kenny has a bottomless pit of a stomach.

When we got to the camp fire, everyone else was already there. The M&Ms looked at us suspiciously, but we just ignored them. As Teletubbies were on cooking duty, it was their job to hand round the food. Fortunately Regina Hill gave us ours, so we weren't too worried about the M&Ms tampering with it in some way first!

We were each given a piece of silver foil, which was a bit weird. But it made sense when we were given two slices of buttered bread and some thin pieces of cheese. We had to put one piece of bread butter side down on the foil, put on the cheese, then the other piece of bread, butter side up. Then we folded the silver paper round it like a parcel and gave it to Snowy Owl to shove into the embers of the fire. The sandwiches cooked for five minutes then she turned them over and after another five minutes they were ready. Scrum-mee!

After we'd eaten, Brown Owl reminded us that as it was our last night we would all be performing something round the camp fire. We had totally forgotten about it, so we went into a mega-panic.

"We'll just have to work on one of our dance routines," said Frankie.

"But when will we have time?" asked Fliss. "We're orienteering round the whole of Foxton Glen this afternoon. It's going to take ages."

"We'll just have to practise our dance between the control points," said Kenny.

And that's just what we did. We must have looked crazy doing our All Saints meets the Spice Girls routines next to the climbing wall and across the archery field. We had to sing, too, which made it difficult because we were all singing at slightly different speeds. We're used to doing our routines to proper cassettes – singing along at the same time isn't as easy as you'd think.

"This is never going to work!" grumbled Fliss. "Everyone's going to laugh at us."

"Not if they know what's good for them!" warned Kenny. "Which reminds me, I've got this little baby here to take care of." She pulled the teddy she had stolen from the M&Ms tent out of her pocket.

"What are you going to do with it?" asked Rosie.

"I'll show you," Kenny replied.

We were standing next to the frog pond. Overhanging it there was a tall straggly bush.

"There we go!" laughed Kenny, leaning over and wedging the bear between some of its branches.

"Should we leave the M&Ms a ransom note or something?" I asked Kenny.

"Then they'd know it was us who'd stolen it, wouldn't they?" said Fliss, looking all panicky. "And we'd get into trouble."

"But so would the M&Ms, because if they dobbed us in to Brown Owl, we'd have to tell her about them sneaking into our tent and stealing our midnight feast," reasoned Kenny.

That was certainly true, but it still seemed a bit risky.

"What should we put in the note?" asked Rosie. "We can't really ask for money or anything, can we?"

"We should call a truce until after the Assault Course Challenge tomorrow," suggested Frankie. She's always very sensible.

"Then if we win, we know that we've won fair and square!" I laughed.

"What do you mean *if* we win," shouted Kenny. "Of course we're going to win. Now – race you to the next control point!"

Unfortunately, we were heading for the dreaded Blue Peter. We hadn't been near it since the first day and Fliss nearly flipped when she saw it again. She went all white and trembly. I really thought she was going to pass out.

"Come on, Fliss," I reassured her. "Remember what we said – you're as capable as anyone of competing tomorrow. Just take it a bit at a time."

Snowy Owl was waiting on the assault course, because you're not allowed on it without an adult there. She could see that Fliss was in a state, and encouraged her to go on it for a few minutes to conquer her fear. Fliss just didn't want to be there, but of course she was under heavy pressure from the rest of us to give it a go. I felt really sorry for her actually. But she did OK – she even got over the scramble nets.

But then, as usual, Kenny went and totally

destroyed her confidence. "We'll never win if you're such a snail," she yelled. "Hurry up, for goodness' sake!"

Fliss froze and couldn't carry on. The rest of us were furious with Kenny.

"Shut up!" Frankie yelled at her. "Fliss is doing her best. We're sick of you telling us what to do! I don't know why you don't just leave us alone."

Oh no! Not again! It was awful. Frankie and Rosie comforted Fliss, who slid down the rope swing and said she couldn't carry on. Kenny went off in a sulk by herself and I had to try to pretend to Snowy Owl that everything was all fine and dandy!

How we finished the orienteering without a major punch-up, I'll never know. But worse than that was having to perform together in the show around the camp fire that evening. We'd hardly practised anything and we weren't speaking to Kenny. Well, I was, but the others weren't. And we hadn't had the chance to tell the M&Ms that we'd kidnapped one of their teddy bears. But that was the least of our worries.

The camp fire itself was mega-cool. Or it would have been if we'd been our normal Sleepover Club selves. As it was, we felt that there was a huge rift between us all. If we were supposed to be Rugrats, then Kenny was definitely Angelica, bossing the rest of us around. So when we were getting our jacket potatoes ready and preparing our billie-cans for apple crisp, Kenny sat a little way from us, muttering to herself.

We had a good laugh anyway because the stupid M&Ms greased the inside of their billie-cans with Fairy Liquid, instead of the outside. So when they started cooking over the camp fire all their ingredients were soapy and frothing inside. Yeuch!

While our potatoes were baking and the apple crisp was cooling, we put on the show. Each patrol took it in turns to perform for the others. We were dreading it, but nothing could have prepared us for what happened next.

It started off OK. The girls from the

Wombles sang a really funny song called 'What's the Use of Wearing Braces', then The Simpsons told a really spooky ghost story about some Guides who got lost at camp, which made us go all goosepimply and huddle together. We wanted to get ours over with, but no, Emma Hughes insisted that Teletubbies went next. Can you guess what they did? Pretended to be Teletubbies, of course. How original! In Amanda Porter's case it didn't take too much imagination. She was already bright red all over and her hair stands up in a funny curl, so she was a dead-ringer for Po!

When it was finally our turn, we decided to sing and do a routine to 'I Know Where It's At'. We were pretty sure that Kenny didn't want to join in, so Frankie said, "There's just the four of us, because Kenny's not feeling very well." She flashed a look at Kenny, who flashed it right back.

"I'm feeling very well, thank you," she said. "I'm joining in, too."

Frankie rolled her eyes at the rest of us

and we all took up our positions. Kenny made sure that she was right at the front. Frankie counted us in and we were off. To start with we were all singing at different times, and I could see the M&Ms and their silly friends spluttering behind their hands. That of course made Kenny really mad, and suddenly she took off into this crazy dance routine which we'd never practised before. The rest of us carried on singing and dancing as best we could, but Kenny was the centre of everyone's attention. And I have to admit she was pretty amazing.

I don't remember exactly what happened next, it all seemed to happen so fast. Kenny's head must have been in something of a spin because she was moving like a maniac. But she was also dancing pretty close to where the M&Ms were sitting. I'm almost certain that I saw Emma Hughes stick out her foot, and the next thing we knew Kenny had stumbled and was staggering near to the fire. Then she let out a cry. It was a cry like I'd never heard before.

We all rushed over to her. Brown Owl had moved fast when she saw Kenny careering towards the fire, but she hadn't got there fast enough to prevent her from falling.

"Are you all right?" asked Frankie anxiously, looking at Kenny who was sprawled on the ground.

"My ankle hurts," Kenny replied, grimacing with pain.

Brown Owl bent down and checked it over carefully. "Well you haven't broken it," she told her, "but you've sprained it quite badly. I'll bandage it up now and then your father can look at it when you get home tomorrow."

You know that Kenny's dad's a doctor, don't you? And Kenny is fascinated by all that medical stuff, too, so she was in her element, even if she did look as white as a sheet. Everybody was crowding round her, the M&Ms as well, and Emma Hughes had a particularly nasty smirk on her face.

When Brown Owl had bandaged Kenny's ankle, Frankie and I helped her up and supported her as she hopped over to the nearest log.

"*I* was sitting there!" said Emily Berryman nastily.

"Well you'll just have to sit somewhere else, won't you!" said Snowy Owl coolly. "And I want you to look after Kenny and make sure that she has everything she needs."

That made Kenny laugh out loud. "I'm going to enjoy this!" she told us, as she made Emma Hughes fetch her potato from the fire. Then, what with one thing and another, she made them run about after her all evening. We were in stitches watching them scurrying about like ants. Especially as you could tell that they were hating every minute of it!

It was only later when we were finally in bed – it had taken Kenny hours to get to the toilet block and back – that we realised just how much Kenny's injury was going to affect us.

"What about the Blue Peter Challenge?"

asked Rosie suddenly. "How are we going to compete in it now?"

All the colour drained from Kenny's face. I really thought she was going to cry.

CHAPTER NINE

"The Assault Course Challenge!" Kenny kept moaning. "I was determined to win it and now I can't even take part!"

The rest of us looked at each other. I felt desperately sorry for Kenny, but I couldn't think of anything to say which would make her feel better.

"Maybe I can still compete in it," said Kenny, sounding brighter. "If I'm careful I should be all right."

"Don't be stupid!" Frankie said. "You'd only do yourself more damage." She looked at the rest of us, then back at Kenny. "I know you've been driving us crazy about this whole Challenge thing," Frankie continued, "but as it's so important to you, we'll try to win it for you, as a sort of get-well present!"

Fliss didn't look too sure about that. "But I can't do it," she wailed, her eyes filling with tears. "What if I let you down?"

"You can do it and you won't let us down!" Kenny told her. "You just need confidence. And I'll be there to cheer you on!"

Now that didn't sound like a good idea at all.

"I won't be having a go, I promise!" she reassured us. "And I'm not going to say this again, but I'm sorry about getting carried away before. I hate falling out with you guys!"

We all gave each other a group hug round the tent pole.

"Crikey, that was like something out of 'Friends'!" laughed Kenny and we all collapsed into giggles. Apart from me. I collapsed into hiccups.

"Lyndz, you do pick your moments!"

laughed Frankie, digging her thumb into my palm.

"I'm… hic… sorry!" I giggled.

Suddenly there was an enormous thumping on the side of our tent.

"Oi! You! Have you been into our tent?" It was Emma Hughes.

"And stolen our midnight feast?" asked Amanda Porter.

"That was *our* midnight feast, I think you'll find!" replied Kenny.

"Well you must have stolen teddy Egbert, too," snivelled Emily Berryman. "And I want him back."

"Can't baby sleep without her 'ickle bear then?" asked Rosie in a babyish voice.

"You've stolen him and I'm going to tell Brown Owl!" The Goblin sounded very upset.

"Go ahead and we'll tell her about you stealing our things," said Kenny. "And I'll tell her how you tripped me up, Hughesy. You could have damaged me for life!"

There was silence. Then a few seconds

later we heard Brown Owl. "Really, Emma, I thought you would've known better than to be prowling about at this time of night. Get back to your tent, now. I don't want to hear another sound out of you!"

We waited until she'd gone, then started laughing.

"It's not often those two get into trouble!" laughed Fliss. "They're usually such goody-goodies!"

"It serves them right," I laughed. "And hey, my hiccups have gone! It must have been the shock."

"Well that calls for a celebration!" said Kenny and fished out the sweets from the bottom of her sleeping bag. "Here's to being friends again!"

We toasted each other with fizzy cola sweets.

"And to beating the M&Ms in the Assault Course Challenge!" I said. But as soon as I'd said it, I wished I hadn't. Fliss began to look very troubled again.

"Fliss, you'll be brilliant!" Kenny

reassured her and she sounded serious. You could tell that it meant a lot to Fliss to hear Kenny say that. In fact it really cheered her up. And whose idea do you think it was to do a conga round our sleeping bags at one in the morning? Right, Miss Sidebotham herself. I fell asleep when the others started to sing 'Wannabe', doing all the dance moves in their sleeping bags, and Frankie told me they didn't get to sleep until after three!

You could tell that they'd had a late night because I was the only one who was wide awake at seven o'clock. The others were all bleary-eyed and moany. Not the best start to a day when the reputation of the Sleepover Club was on the line!

"Come on, guys!" I yelled at them. "We've an important day ahead of us!"

They all groaned and staggered out of their sleeping bags, and they didn't seem to wake up properly until after they'd eaten breakfast. It was a good thing they woke up then because we had the craziest time after that. We had to pack all our stuff away and take our bags to the minibus, then we had to help the rangers take down the tents and make sure the camp fire had been put out properly. There was just so much work for three nights of camping, but it had been worth it. And of course the real highlight – for us anyway – was still to come. Yep, it was finally time for the long-awaited Assault Course Challenge.

We all lined up at the start of the course and Brown Owl explained a few things to us. "Now, there'll only be four girls competing from each patrol," she said. "Kenny has an injured ankle and one girl from each of the other patrols has told me that she's not keen on taking part in the Challenge either. Those girls are now managers and official cheerleaders!"

Kenny led the cheering and Fliss looked furious. "If you hadn't hurt your stupid ankle, I wouldn't have had to compete in this after all!" she hissed to Kenny.

"Now, as there are two sets of obstacles

and four teams, Jerry and I are going to be timing each team. The Challenge is going to be based on the overall time each patrol takes to complete the course," continued Brown Owl, "so you're not just competing against the team next to you, you're competing against the times of the other teams as well. Do you all understand?"

Everyone nodded.

"I hope we're not teamed against the stupid M&Ms," I whispered to Frankie.

"Right, listen up," said Brown Owl. "The Simpsons and the Wombles will be competing together and Teletubbies will be teamed against Rugrats."

We all groaned.

"Just our luck!" said Rosie.

"So if those of you taking part for The Simpsons and Wombles can line up here, we'll get started!"

We moved away from the starting line, which was pretty crowded. Everybody seemed to be deciding on who was going to go first from each team. The M&Ms were skulking around, too.

"So which of you has wimped out then?" Kenny asked them.

Amanda Porter went bright red.

"Well that's no surprise, is it? You're so big you'd probably get stuck in the underground tunnel!" laughed Fliss.

I don't like people being criticised just because they're a bit bigger than everybody else, especially as Fliss once did that to me. But Amanda Porter is truly awful, so she deserved it.

"Where's my bear, anyway, you thieving little snakes?" asked Emily Berryman.

"You'll only see it again if you agree to play fair in this challenge," Frankie told them firmly. "If you try to pull any stunts, your bear will be a dead ted. Understood?"

The Goblin looked shocked. She looked round at her friends and they all, reluctantly, nodded.

"OK then. May the best team win!" laughed Kenny.

We went back to join everybody else at

the start of the course.

There was a lot of cheering as the first two teams set off. The Wombles were awesome. A girl called Rachel Sunderland went off first for them. She was like a real little monkey swinging her way over all the obstacles.

"Wow! Look at her go!" cooed Kenny. "I hope you're all taking notes!"

Fliss started jiggling up and down. I could sense how nervous she was. With the next two girls, The Simpsons started catching up a bit, so by the time the fourth competitors were going over the obstacles it was really tight.

The Wombles last competitor was Hannah Williams. We knew her from school and she's brilliant at games, in fact she's the captain of our netball team. She flew over the scramble nets as though they weren't there. It was amazing.

"We'll never beat their time!" I said.

"Yes we will!" Kenny told us confidently. "Right, we're on. Lyndz, you go first to give us a good start, then Fliss, then Frankie. Rosie, you're last, so you've got to be prepared to do the business for us!"

We all huddled together.

"Do this for me!" Kenny told us. "And let's whip the pants off those stupid M&Ms!"

We all broke away and did a high five.

"Pathetic!" spat Emma Hughes.

"We'll soon see who's pathetic!" said Kenny knowingly.

Then it was my turn to go.

As soon as Brown Owl blew her whistle I charged down the course. I could hear Kenny yelling, but I wouldn't let myself look at her. I raced over the hurdle and balanced on the log without falling in. It was wicked! I felt like I was flying. It was almost as good as galloping on a horse.

"Come on, Lyndz! You're miles ahead!" shouted Kenny. "Regina Hill's rubbish!"

By the time I had crawled through the tunnel and back over the scramble nets, I knew that I was way in front. It was a great feeling swinging across the ditch on the rope swing, I could have done it all day. But there were more important things to think about. I just had the swinging tyres to negotiate, before handing over to Fliss. I could see her at the line waiting for me. I'll never forget her face. She was dead white and looked as though she was about to throw up. I whizzed through the tyre swing and threw myself at the line.

"It's a piece of cake, Fliss. You're way ahead, just enjoy yourself!" I panted.

Fliss didn't look capable of enjoying herself, but as soon as I'd touched her hand she set off. We all held our breath. This was Fliss's moment to shine, if only her nerves didn't get the better of her.

CHAPTER TEN

Now, I have to tell you that from the start it didn't look good for Fliss. It took her about three attempts to get over the hurdle, and that wasn't even high. I thought she was going to have kittens when she had to run across the log and risk falling in the mud underneath.

"Come on, for goodness' sake," Kenny was muttering under her breath. "Alana 'Banana' is catching up."

"You're doing great, Fliss," I shouted. "Take your time and you'll be fine." And don't look at Kenny's angry mush, I wanted to add.

"You've got to encourage her," I told Kenny. "That's what Fliss responds to."

Kenny tutted and shouted, "Great Fliss! It's running through the tyres next and that's no problem."

Actually, it really wasn't a problem. Fliss is so light and nimble that she just danced through them as though they weren't there.

"Great stuff!" Kenny and I cheered.

Alana 'Banana' had fallen off the log twice by now and was looking really muddy and fed-up. Fliss was way in front. But the dreaded scramble nets were looming.

"OK, Fliss, take your time!" I shouted. "Just think about a wobbly fence, that's all it is!"

Fliss's face was a picture of concentration. You could almost hear her grit her teeth as she put her head down and went for it. Snowy Owl was at the bottom of the net shouting encouragement. But I think it was Kenny shouting "The M&Ms are watching Fliss, show 'em what you're made of!" which really inspired her. She shinned up the nets like Catwoman and threw herself over the top. It was awesome.

"Way to go, Fliss!" Kenny and I shouted, leaping about like lunatics. "You're miles ahead, just keep going."

Everything else after that was a piece of cake. It was as though Fliss had totally conquered her fears and was really enjoying herself. When she got to the second lot of scramble nets she climbed up them like she'd been doing it all her life. Was this really our wimpy Fliss? Maybe the real one had been abducted by aliens and this was an extra-terrestrial replacement! But why should we care? We were beating Teletubbies by miles.

There was one sticky moment when she lost her grip on the rope swing and had to have two attempts to get over the ditch. But by that stage it didn't matter because she was so far ahead of Alana 'Banana' anyway.

We were virtually hysterical by the time Fliss ran home. Of course Frankie and Rosie still had to go over the assault course, but we weren't worried about them. We were home and dry – or so we thought!

The first thing to go wrong was that Frankie wasn't quite ready when Fliss ran home. I think she'd expected her to take much longer and she was still tying up her shoelace when Fliss appeared. Because of that, she didn't take full advantage of the lead our team had over Teletubbies. And she was up against Emma Hughes.

At least Frankie had me, Kenny and Fliss cheering her on. We ran the length of the course yelling encouragement. Fliss was still all hyper and kept shouting how 'easy' everything was, which was a bit of a laugh considering what she's normally like. I don't think Frankie appreciated it too much, either. Especially when she got her foot caught in the scramble netting and was hanging almost upside down for a few seconds.

Emma Hughes didn't have much support at all. Amanda Porter was too fat to keep running alongside her, Alana 'Banana' was too traumatised after her experiences, Regina Hill was exhausted and Emily Berryman was waiting next to Rosie at the starting line. Still, you could tell that Emma Hughes was desperate not to be beaten by us and she raced with Frankie right to the line. So when it came to Rosie's turn, she and Emily Berryman were neck and neck.

My heart was in my mouth as they raced over the first few obstacles. But at the first scramble net it became obvious that this was going to be no contest. Berryman was green with fear – she just couldn't hack it. My friends are always telling me that I'm too soft on people, but I felt really sorry for her, even if she is one of our deadly rivals.

The noise on the course was just crazy because all the other teams were cheering as well. Rosie and Emily were the last competitors in the Blue Peter Challenge and the whole contest would be decided on their times.

"Easy-peasy, Rosie!" yelled Kenny as Rosie flew over the top of the nets. "No contest, man! The Goblin's gone to pieces."

I could sense Rosie hesitate as she looked back to where Emily was struggling. But Kenny urged her on and she ran on to the underground tunnel while her competitor was still struggling over the top of the nets.

"She's miles ahead and I bet we're faster than those Wombles, too!" laughed Kenny. "I'm going to ask Brown Owl what their time was."

She hobbled off to the finishing line where Brown Owl was standing with her stopwatch, and she didn't see that Rosie was slowing down. Emily Berryman had crawled out of the underground tunnel and looked as though she was going to throw up again. Emma Hughes was yelling at her to carry on. Her face was all screwed up in anger – not a pretty sight!

Rosie had heard all the commotion behind her as she started to climb the second set of scramble nets. She looked back and saw that Emily Berryman was in difficulties. You could tell that she really didn't know what to do.

Frankie, Fliss and I were yelling like demons so Rosie carried on climbing to the top of her net. She was just about to swing herself over when Emily started crying below her. She was clinging to the net and unable to move. Without thinking, Rosie climbed back down and said something to her, then they slowly climbed the nets together. Rosie watched Emily climb over the top first then she swung herself over. When she'd checked that Berryman was OK, she leapt down and ran like crazy. She hurled herself at the rope swing then sprinted on to the tyre swing, which was the last obstacle.

"What were you doing?" Kenny screamed at her as she crossed the line. "We were miles in front and then you threw it away. You lost us the Challenge to help one of the M&Ms of all people!" She spat the accusation out as though it was the most disgusting thing she could think of.

Rosie was still out of breath. "I'm sorry,"

she panted, "but I could see how frightened she was. I couldn't just leave her there, could I?"

"I would've done!" snarled Kenny. "Wombles only won by thirty seconds. That's thirty seconds, Rosie. You lost us that by going back to help that stupid dead-head! Some get-well present that turned out to be!"

Kenny limped off angrily and poor Rosie looked distraught. "I didn't know what to do!" she kept saying, over and over again.

When it came to the prize ceremony we couldn't bear to watch. The trophy for the winners was all gold and shiny. We'd have loved to have been the ones raising it up as though it was the World Cup.

"So near and yet so far!" muttered Frankie.

Then Brown Owl surprised us all. "We usually only have one prize in this Challenge," she told us all seriously. "But I think what we saw today deserves another one. Rosie, in the Rugrats' team, demonstrated what being in the Brownies and Guides is all about – taking the initiative to help other people even if it sometimes means losing out yourself. Today Rugrats lost the Blue Peter Challenge because of Rosie's actions. But I'm going to create a special Sportsmanship Award, and Rugrats will be the first team to receive it."

We all went wild, and everybody else was cheering us, too. Apart from the M&Ms of course! Kenny actually started to smile again and soon she was back to her normal noisy self, laughing and larking around.

Before leaving the campsite we went to retrieve Egbert, Emily Berryman's teddy bear. It wasn't as easy to get down from the bush as it had been to put up there, but we managed to hook it towards us with a stick. Kenny took great pleasure in throwing it at the M&Ms when we got on the minibus.

"Here's your bear!" she snarled. "You should've put him in your team for the Blue Peter Challenge. He'd have been better than you were, Berryman!"

Emily Berryman went bright red and looked as though she was going to cry.

Emma Hughes just looked furious.

Just to annoy the M&Ms even more we sang 'We Are The Champions' at the top of our voices for most of the way home.

Until Emma Hughes said nastily, "But you're not champions, are you? I don't see any trophy."

Surprisingly, it was Fliss, of all people, who said, "Well, we would've been if your team hadn't been a complete bunch of wimps who needed rescuing every five minutes!"

We all screamed with laughter when she said that. Emma Hughes blushed the colour of a beetroot and Emily Berryman looked as though she wished she could slip through a hole in the minibus floor.

We haven't actually got our award yet. We won't be getting it until we go back to Brownies next term. Brown Owl says she's going to have a trophy made, which is well cool. Especially as ours will be the first names on it. Kenny keeps telling us that the trophy is really hers because we said our performance in the Blue Peter Challenge was her get-well present. I don't think we meant it quite like that though.

Kenny's ankle is much better now, by the way. Her dad said she shouldn't run about on it too much so we keep threatening to wheel her about in a pram. She doesn't seem too keen on that idea. I can't think why!

Going back to our trophy – we can't wait to see it and we're all totally blissed about it, but winning trophies isn't the most important thing in life, is it? I mean, even if we didn't win the Assault Course Challenge we all had a brilliant time at camp. And in some ways we'd all changed a little when we came home. We all seem to have learnt a bit about ourselves. Fliss is still boring us stupid about her triumph of course, but at least Kenny hasn't been teasing her quite so much as she did before.

We're nearly at the playground now. Can you see it, just at the corner of the street?

Everyone's there by the look of it. Fliss seems to be recreating her exploits on the assault course for about the hundredth time. And Kenny looks as though she's about to swing for her. Come on, we'd better hurry up and join Frankie and Rosie in trying to keep the peace. It doesn't look as though our reputation for good sportsmanship is going to last that long, does it?!

Sleepover Girls

go Detective

by Louis Catt

Collins

An imprint of HarperCollins*Publishers*

CHAPTER ONE

Hello – and I'm very pleased to see you. I'd like to welcome you to the Sleepover Club.

There! Isn't that better than Frankie or Kenny? They just jump straight into the story, and my mum says you should *always* be polite. The others tease me because I don't really like rushing about the way they do – but I think *someone* has to be sensible, don't you? My mum says that sometimes the others get too wild, and she doesn't like me to be like that. Sometimes it *is* funny, though. I mean, when we were pretending to be yowling cats outside Mrs Brierley's house and she threw a bucket of water over Frankie and Rosie... but I shouldn't be telling you that now. (Don't worry – I won't forget to tell you all the details when I get to that bit in the story!)

Perhaps I should have started by saying "How do you do?" Or maybe that's too much? Anyway, I'm Felicity Diana Sidebotham, and I'm ten. I'm the oldest in the Sleepover Club. My birthday is September 16th; I used to mind, because it meant I was always the oldest in the class, but I don't mind so much now. I rather like it.

If you want to know what I look like I've got really truly blonde hair, and I'm very slim. My mum says I've got a very good figure, and she ought to know. She's a beautician. It's nice having a mum who knows about hair and beauty things; my mum is always careful about what she eats, and I am too. I don't want to get fat. *Gross!*

I live with my mum and my stepdad, Andy, and I've got a little brother called Callum. Sometimes he's OK, but sometimes I wish he was a girl. If he was a girl I could talk to him about clothes and things. My real dad got married to someone else and they've got a lovely little baby girl, but she's much too young to talk to. She's very pretty, though. My mum says I'm pretty too, but sometimes I'm not sure. It's difficult to tell when you look at your own face in the mirror. When Callum wants to wind me up he says my nose is like a great big squashed tomato, but I don't think it is. Not really. It's just Callum being a boy.

Don't you think girls are much nicer than boys? I mostly do – except for Ryan Scott. He's in our class at school. He's a brilliant footballer, and he's very interesting to talk to. Well, that's what I think – although Frankie and Kenny and Lyndz and Rosie just laugh when I say so. My mum says they're jealous because he likes me better than them, but I don't think they really care.

Do you know the other members of the Sleepover Club? There's Frankie and Kenny – they're best friends. Actually, sometimes – just between you and me – I feel a tiny bit left out when we're at school. And sometimes I even feel like that when we're having a sleepover. Frankie and Kenny get on really well together, and they love playing tricks, and I don't. Once they put pretend blood all over Kenny's garden path, and I thought it was real… I nearly fainted! My knees went completely wobbly and I felt swimmy in my head and Rosie said afterwards that my face went green. Kenny had to get me hot sugary tea, and wrap me up in a duvet. Did you know that's what you do if someone has a bad shock? Kenny wants to be a doctor when she grows up, so she's good at knowing things like that. Her dad's a doctor.

Oh! I'm not being very organised. I hope you're not muddled! I'll go back to the beginning and tell you about the others properly.

Frankie first. She doesn't have any brothers or sisters. She's got a pet dog called Pepsi, though. I like Pepsi because she isn't the sort of dog who jumps up and puts her muddy paws all over you. A long time ago Frankie had a cat called Muffin who got run over, and if you think it's odd that I'm telling you about a dead cat, it isn't. If Frankie hadn't still been missing Muffin she wouldn't have— *whoops*! I keep forgetting that this is the introduction, and I mustn't tell you too much of the story yet. Perhaps you could just remember about Muffin, though.

Then there's Kenny. Like I told you, she wants to be a doctor. She's got two sisters, and she has to share her bedroom with her sister Molly. I'm really glad I don't have to share with anyone. Molly is *horrible* – we call her Molly the Monster. She's always complaining about Kenny – although I do think Kenny is a bit untidy. If you look under her bed you'll see it's *stuffed* with dirty clothes. There's even a big bag of rat food – UGH!!! Luckily the rat is in the garage. I don't think I'd ever be able to sleep over at Kenny's house if the rat was in her room like she wants it to be. I'd have terrible dreams about scaly tails and horrible sharp teeth all night long.

I haven't told you about Lyndz and Rosie

yet. Rosie is like me; she doesn't live with her dad. She's got a big sister, Tiffany, and an older brother called Adam who uses a wheelchair. Her house is a bit like Lyndz's house; it's very messy and a lot of the walls need painting. Rosie says her dad keeps promising he'll come back and sort it out, but he doesn't. I don't think I'd like to have Rosie's room at all. My bedroom has ever such pretty wallpaper, and my mum let me choose my curtains and my rug.

Who haven't I told you about yet? Oh yes – Lyndz. She's got two brothers who are older than her, and two younger ones. She lives in a big untidy house with things all over it, and her dad is always doing stuff to it. I think they should ask my stepdad, Andy, to do it properly (he's a very neat plasterer) but they don't. It's odd, but they seem to like it just the way it is... and I suppose it is sort of comfortable. You never have to worry about spilling things or keeping the cushions all nice and puffed up like we do in my house. Lyndz has a dog, but I don't like him as much as

Frankie's. He barks all the time, and he rushes about. Sometimes he jumps on your lap, and his paws are all wet and muddy and disgusting. There are three cats too... Toffee, Fudge and Truffle. It was because of Truffle that we turned into detectives... because one day Truffle went missing!

CHAPTER TWO

When Truffle disappeared, Lyndz was really upset. She was late arriving at school, and her eyes were red. Mrs Weaver – our teacher – told her that cats often wander off on their own for a bit, but Lyndz said Truffle *always* comes in at six o'clock for her kitty crunchies.

"When did you last see her?" Frankie asked.

"Yesterday morning," Lyndz said, and she sniffed loudly. "She was licking the butter and I shouted at her. Maybe she's run away because I was so horrible."

"*Yeah!*" The M&Ms grinned at each other. "Cruel – that's what you are! *Poor* little pussy.

She's run away to live with people who will be kind to her!"

Have I told you about the M&Ms? Their real names are Emma Hughes and Emily Berryman, and they hate us and we hate them. They're always trying to get one up on us – sometimes they are just so mean.

This time it looked as if they'd been really successful. Lyndz turned her back on them, but I could see her shoulders were shaking. She was blowing her nose really hard. I glared at the M&Ms, and so did Kenny.

"If you think it's funny making jokes about someone's lost cat you're even grosser than we thought you were!" Kenny said.

The M&Ms tried not to grin, but they couldn't quite stop. Lyndz went on worrying. "It was so cold last night, too," she wailed. "Truffle *never* stays out all night. She sleeps on the end of my bed, and keeps my toes warm."

Frankie put her arm round Lyndz's shoulders just as one of the M&Ms whispered to the other, and they fell about shrieking with laughter.

"What's so funny?" Frankie asked them.

They didn't answer, but went on giggling.

Frankie went right up to them, and Kenny went with her.

"Tell us what the joke is!" Frankie said, and she sounded terribly fierce.

Emma stopped laughing. "We were only fooling around," she said. "I'm sorry if you're worried."

They didn't look sorry at all. "Cats are always going off," Emily said. "Our cat goes out every night." She began to snigger again. "We were wondering if your mum thought your cat was a hot water bottle and hung it up in a cupboard!" And then they both laughed all over again.

I wanted to tell Mrs Weaver, but Lyndz said it wasn't worth it. She said we'd always known the M&Ms were totally pathetic, and the way they were going on just proved it.

"Take no notice of them," Rosie said. "If we do it'll only make them worse."

I think Rosie was right. She knows quite a lot about how to treat people; I think it might be because sometimes stupid people call her brother names.

The bell went then, and we had to go back into lessons. Mrs Weaver was very nice to Lyndz, which was just as well as Lyndz got all her spellings wrong.

Halfway through the afternoon I saw Frankie pass Lyndz a note.

Lyndz read it (Mrs Weaver was writing something on the board) and then she passed it on to me. It said:

HEY! I'VE HAD AN IDEA! IF TRUFFLE ISN'T AT HOME TONIGHT SOMEONE MUST HAVE STOLEN HER... SO WE'LL BE THE SLEEPOVER DETECTIVES AND TRACK HER DOWN!!!!

I looked at Lyndz, and she was sitting up much straighter and smiling at Frankie. I passed the note on to Rosie, and she read it too. Then Kenny got it, and she said "YES!" so loudly that Mrs Weaver turned round.

"Am I missing something?" she asked.

We all tried to look as if we had been

17

working extra specially hard. Of course the M&Ms had to blurt.

"They were passing notes, Mrs Weaver," Emma said, and she gave us a huge fat horrible smile.

"That's right, Mrs Weaver," Emily said. "We both saw them."

Now, Mrs Weaver usually hates us passing notes more than anything else. She says it's underhand, and that if we have something to say we should stand up and say it. She says it is really rude, and means we don't respect her at all. This time, though, she gave Emma and Emily a funny look.

"Thank you," she said. "If ever I want a report on the private activities in my class I'll remember to ask you two. In the meantime, however, I suggest you all get on with what you're doing."

That squashed the M&Ms! We could hardly believe our luck. We put our heads down and worked really hard until the end of the lesson – which was also going-home time.

When we'd cleared up and put our chairs

on the tables, Frankie went straight up to Mrs Weaver. She was holding the note in her hand. She walked right past the M&Ms, and I saw them staring.

"I'm sorry, Mrs Weaver," Frankie said, "but I did pass Lyndz a note. It wasn't a bad one, though. You can read it – I just wanted to cheer her up."

Mrs Weaver smiled at Frankie, and dropped the note in the wastepaper basket.

"I had a feeling it was something like that," she said. "Don't do it again, though." And she went on clearing up, still smiling.

The M&Ms looked as sick as parrots!!!

When we got outside the school gate Frankie let out a loud "WHOOPEE!!!" and we all joined in. Then Kenny said we should give three cheers for Mrs Weaver, so we did that too. (I think it was a little bit louder than it might have been because the M&Ms were walking past exactly at that moment!)

Then Frankie grabbed Lyndz's arm. "Can you ring us if Truffle's still missing?" she asked her. "And if she is we'll make a Grand Plan!"

"Sleepover Detectives!" Rosie said, and she whacked Lyndz on the back in an encouraging sort of way.

Kenny giggled. "We can't catnap if we're looking for a catnapper," she said.

"But we'll catch the catnapper who's napping with the cat!" Frankie said.

"We can pore over her paw prints and follow the trail to her tail!" Rosie chipped in.

We all laughed then, even Lyndz.

"I'll ring as soon as I get home," she promised.

I'd been thinking while the others were telling jokes. (I'm not very good at being funny.) I wasn't sure what we could do if we were detectives; I was worrying that we didn't have things like magnifying glasses and cameras, and all the other things detectives need.

"What exactly will we do?" I asked. "I mean, if she hasn't come home? Where will we look first?"

Frankie stopped grinning and rubbed her nose. "Maybe we should check out the pet shop. Maybe someone might have found her and thought she was a stray."

"Wouldn't they take her to a cats' home?" Kenny said. "Or the RSPCA?"

"She's got our phone number on her collar," Lyndz said, and she began to look unhappy again. "If someone had found her they'd have rung up."

"Could she have lost her collar?" I asked. Rosie nodded.

"Our cat wriggles out of his quite often. It's because you mustn't put their collars on too tight."

"She might have lost it," Lyndz said. "Actually, it was a bit loose, and it had one of those elasticky bits on it."

"Well then!" Kenny waved her arms in the air. "Probably she got stuck in a tree or something yesterday, and she wriggled out of her collar this morning—"

"And she's sitting on your bed at home now this minute!" Rosie yelled.

Lyndz smiled at us. "Thanks," she said. "I do feel better now."

"Will you ring us anyway, even if she's back?" I asked.

"Of course I will." Lyndz picked up her bag. "I'll zoom back and see right this minute." She dashed off, and we all went home too.

CHAPTER THREE

I'd only been at home about ten minutes when the phone rang. It wasn't Lyndz – it was Frankie. She said Lyndz's mum had told Lyndz she could only ring two of us and we were to pass the message on. Anyway, Frankie said Truffle was still missing, and we were all going to go to the pet shop after school tomorrow.

"We could come back to my house afterwards to make a plan if Truffle's not there," I said.

"Actually," Frankie said, "everyone's coming to my house. I've already arranged it. Oh, and

Lyndz's mum says she can have a sleepover at her house next Friday to cheer her up… or if Truffle's back it can be a celebration! OK?"

"Yes," I said. "All right."

"See you tomorrow, then," Frankie said, and she rang off.

I put the phone down too. Sometimes Frankie can be very bossy. We hardly ever meet up after school at my house, and my house is much the nicest. My mum really likes it when everyone come round too, and she makes us special cakes and buys lots of different kinds of biscuits.

We had to wait for my brother Callum before we could go to the pet shop the next day. He walks home with me, and my mum says he's not old enough to come home on his own. His class was late coming out; because they're younger they seem to take ages and ages getting their coats on.

While we were waiting, Lyndz told us she'd been doing some detective work on her own.

"The last person who saw Truffle was Mum," she said. "Truffle was bouncing out of the cat flap, and she looked just like she always does. And we've checked all the cupboards and sheds and drawers, because a friend of Mum's said her cat got into her airing cupboard and was shut in for six days while they were away on holiday!"

"Was the cat OK?" Rosie asked.

Lyndz nodded. "Yes. It was very thin, but it was completely fine as soon as it had had something to eat!"

Kenny was looking thoughtful. "What did the airing cupboard look like?"

I knew exactly what she was going to ask about. Kenny always wants to know about disgusting things. Luckily just at that moment Callum came round the corner, so I jumped up.

"Look!" I said. "There's Callum! Let's go!"

Callum was a bit grumpy about having to go to the pet shop, but he cheered up when Lyndz told him about Truffle. She's got younger brothers too, so she knows how to talk to him.

"I'll look out for her," he said. "I'm very good at seeing things."

25

We all squeezed into the pet shop together. It isn't very big, so we more or less filled it up. There were cages all over the walls, and all round the floor too. I didn't mind the ones with birds peeping and cheeping, but I didn't look at the ones with horrible squirmy little rats and mice in.

Mr Garez didn't look very pleased to see us, which is unfair because the customer is always right. Besides, Lyndz buys loads of rat food from his shop, and Frankie's mum buys dog food there.

"I hope you've come for a reason," he said. "I'm fed up with kids coming in just to look at the kittens. This is a shop, not a zoo."

"Kittens!" Kenny said. "Oh, Mr Garez – where are they?"

Mr Garez sighed very loudly and pointed at a big cage in the corner – and there they were. Three tabby kittens, and a tiny fluffy black one that was chasing its tail round and round and round.

"OH!" Frankie nearly fell over her feet in her rush to look closer. "LOOK! He's *exactly* like Muffin!"

"Who's Muffin?" Rosie asked her.

"He was my cat who died," Frankie said. "He was *lovely*, and I still miss him. He was black all over with a tiny white spot under his chin – oh, Mr Garez, *please* can I hold him? Just for a minute?"

Mr Garez sighed again, even louder than before, but he came over to the cage. "He's a little terror, that one," he said as he fished the black kitten out and plopped it into Frankie's hands. "He's forever getting out. I'll be glad when someone takes him."

Frankie was gazing at the kitten, and her eyes were shining. "I'll take him!" she said. "My mum and dad won't mind – we've still got Muffin's food bowl in the cupboard! How much is he?" And she started pulling her purse out of her pocket with one hand while she cuddled the kitten with the other.

Kenny, Rosie, Lyndz and I stared at her.

"Are you sure your mum and dad won't mind?" Rosie said. "I mean, shouldn't you at least go home and ask?"

Frankie shook her head. "I *know* they'll be pleased," she said. "Mum knows how much I miss Muffin, and Pepsi's getting much older now – she'll be thrilled to have another animal to play with!"

"Meow," said the kitten. It was funny! It was just as if he had understood every word Frankie was saying.

Frankie looked desperate. "I *have* to have him!" she said. "LOOK! You can see he knows he belongs with me!"

"Five pounds," said Mr Garez. "The owner said five pounds to a good home."

Frankie tucked the kitten inside her jacket, and opened her purse. "Can anyone lend me a pound?" she asked. "I've only got four – no, four pounds twenty."

We scrabbled about in our pockets. Rosie had ten pence, and Lyndz had fifty. I didn't have any money at all, and neither did Kenny.

Mr Garez watched while we piled up the money on the counter.

"H'm," he said. "Four pounds eighty. Maybe I do a discount for bad kittens," and he actually smiled as he scooped the money up and put it in the till.

"Thank you!" Frankie said. "He'll be the happiest kitten EVER!"

We stroked the little tabby kittens while Mr Garez stumped off into the back of the shop. I wished I could have had one, but Mum says pets aren't hygienic. Also she says they give Callum asthma, although he never gets asthma when he plays with animals at other people's houses.

Mr Garez came back with a piece of paper and a big cardboard box with holes in it.

"Here you are," he said, and he gave Frankie the paper. "He's had all his injections. Feed him four small meals a day, and make sure he has water where he can reach it. Now, pop him in the carrying box to take him home." Mr Garez smiled again. "And don't bring him back! I'm too old to chase him all round the shop five times a day!"

We were just about to walk out when I remembered why we'd come to the shop in the first place.

"Please," I said, "has anyone brought in a lost cat?"

Lyndz jumped round. "Wow, Fliss!" she said. "Well done! How *could* I have forgotten poor old Truffle?"

But Mr Garez said that he hadn't heard anyone talking about a lost cat, and they certainly hadn't brought one in.

"If we write a notice will you put it up in the window?" I asked.

"Of course." Mr Garez seemed really happy now. "Bring it in, and I'll be pleased to do that."

Once we were outside Lyndz gave me a hug. "That's a mega-brilliant idea about the notice," she said. "We'll write a whole lot out at Frankie's house, and ask all the other shops as well. Do you think we could use your dad's computer, Frankie?"

"H'm?" Frankie wasn't listening. She was holding the big cardboard box very very carefully, and was trying to squint in through one of the holes.

"Can we use your computer?" Lyndz asked.

"I expect so," Frankie said. "Dad'll probably

be there when we get back. He and Mum were going out somewhere together this afternoon – don't ask me where. They wouldn't tell me – it seems to be some sort of secret."

"Ooh!" Kenny said. "Tell us more!"

Frankie grinned. "It's something to do with holidays, because when I asked Mum where we were going next summer she looked at Dad, and then he winked at her, and then they both said next summer would be a real surprise... but I'd have to wait for a bit to find out."

"Oh." Kenny sounded disappointed. "Grown ups are so boring."

Rosie suddenly clutched my arm. "FLISS!" she said. "Where's Callum?"

CHAPTER FOUR

We pounded back into the pet shop. My heart was fluttering, but I needn't have worried. Callum was sitting on the counter chatting to Mr Garez – and he was holding a rat!

EEEEEEEEEEEEEEEEEKKKK!!!!!

I didn't mean to scream. It was the surprise – and it was such a BIG rat! It was a fast runner, too. When I screamed the rat and Callum jumped – but the rat jumped higher. Callum and Mr Garez both grabbed at it, and they both missed – and the rat scuttled off at a hundred miles an hour.

"I can see it!" Callum yelled, and he flung

himself on to the floor. He didn't mean to knock over the bag of rabbit food, but it tottered... and then crashed to the floor almost on top of him. Crunchy bits and grassy bits spread absolutely everywhere.

"STOP!!!!!" yelled Mr Garez. "STOP – before I have no shop left!"

Callum froze... and so did the rest of us. I'm sure Frankie and Kenny were completely cracking up laughing, but they hid behind the kitten's cardboard box so Mr Garez couldn't see.

"Now, OUT!" said Mr Garez, and Frankie, Kenny and Rosie zoomed out through the door. Lyndz grabbed Callum's hand, and followed them, and I was going to go too, but I didn't. I really did feel bad about the mess – and after all, Callum is my brother.

I took a deep breath, and I swallowed hard.

"Mr Garez," I said, "I'm *very* sorry."

Mr Garez glared at me. "I should hope so!" he said. "*Look* at all this mess! I should tell your mother!"

"I'll help you sweep it up," I said, and then I

nearly flipped. The rat had come sneaking back out and was nibbling at the rabbit food – and *another* rat had come out too! A HUGE black rat!

I would have screamed again, but I couldn't. My tongue was stuck in my mouth. I couldn't do anything except stare.

Mr Garez swooped down – and picked up both rats – first the brown one, and then the huge black one. Would you believe that he seemed really really pleased to see the black one? He even gave it a little kiss!!! YUCKKKK.

"Aha!" said Mr Garez. "So *there* you are, my pretty friend!"

GROSS!!! Mr Garez had a rat in each hand, and their bristly, scaly tails were twisting round his fingers! I wanted to shut my eyes, but I couldn't.

The rats were soon safely back in their cage, and Mr Garez shut the door with a click. "So – you frighten my rat, young lady, and you spill my rabbit food – but you find me my prize rat while you do it! Maybe we should say that we are quits. And maybe you should go quickly before I change my mind!"

I nodded. I still couldn't say anything. I just headed for the door.

"If your little brother wants a rat," Mr Garez called after me, "I can get him one! Very cheap, too!"

"NO – er – thank you," I called back, and I rushed after the others.

Callum talked about rats all the way back to Frankie's house. The trouble was he'd heard Mr Garez, and he asked me over and over how much 'very cheap' was. I kept telling him to be quiet, but then Kenny told him how great rats are. It's no good, though. My mum would rather have an alien living in the house than a rat. Actually, I think I'd rather have an alien too.

Frankie was right. When we got to her house both her parents were at home. They were sitting have a cup of tea in the kitchen, and they looked – I don't know – pleased with themselves. Anyway, they seemed pleased to see us too, even Callum. Frankie's mum opened a new box of biscuits and her dad put on the kettle.

"So – what ghoulish surprise are you keeping in the box, Frankie?" her dad said as we marched in. "Some horrible sleepover special?"

Frankie went very pink. "Oh, *Dad*!" she said. "It's the most heavenly thing that's happened to me since Muffin died! LOOK!" And she opened the cardboard box.

I don't know what that kitten had been doing in the box. He'd been dead quiet all the way home; not a squeak or a meow. He must have been planning his arrival at Frankie's house. He came out of that box like a furry black streak, and he went straight up the curtains and meowed so loudly you could have heard him six doors down.

Frankie's mum jumped up, and Frankie's dad dropped the milk jug. Callum shouted, and Frankie rushed after the kitten calling, "Muffin! Muff, muff, muff! Don't be frightened!" The kitten jumped; he jumped off the top of the curtains, and he landed on the draining board. It was full of glasses and cups, and he kind of slid along the shiny surface with them... only *they* fell on the floor and he didn't.

"Whoops!" said Rosie, and she ran to head him off, but he did a quick turn and leapt on to the table. Kenny grabbed at him, but he was much too quick. He shot back up the curtains, climbed to the top and hid behind the curtain rail.

"FRANKIE!" said her mum. "*Whatever* is that?"

"He's just scared," Frankie said. "He'll come down in a minute – oh, don't you think he's the most *blissful* kitten in the whole wide world?"

Frankie's dad finished wiping the milk off the floor, and stood up with the wet drippy cloth in his hand.

"I think we should let that animal calm down," he said. "If everyone keeps on chasing it we'll never catch it."

"He'll come down soon," Frankie said. "He's just getting to know us all. Mum, where did we put Muffin's old bowl?"

Frankie's mum looked at her in that way parents do when something is Very Bad News.

"Oh, Frankie!" she said. "Whatever were you thinking of? We *can't* have a kitten – I'm sorry, but there's no way it's possible. I don't know where you got that one from but he'll have to go back."

I felt so sorry for Frankie. I know she's bossy and sometimes she gets too big for her boots and tries to tell us what to do, but anybody would have been sorry for her then. She looked at her dad, and he shook his head.

"Sorry, poppet," he said. "No can do. Wait until he's come down off his mountaineering expedition, and take him home."

"I can't," Frankie said, and there was a wobble in her voice. "Mr Garez said I couldn't. He said he didn't want him back. And," – she looked up at the clock – "his shop is shut now."

"The kitten could come to my house for the night," Lyndz said. "If that would help, that is."

Frankie's mum smiled. "That's very kind of you, Lyndsey – but we can probably manage for tonight." She patted Frankie's hand. "Just don't get too fond of him. I'm not going to change my mind."

Frankie nodded. She didn't say anything, and I think it was because she would have cried if she'd had to open her mouth.

"What were you doing in the pet shop anyway?" asked Frankie's dad. Lyndz had seen Frankie's face too, and she bounced up.

"We were asking about my cat, Truffle," she said. "She's disappeared, and we thought someone might have found her and taken her to the pet shop." She sighed. "But they hadn't."

"There were LOTS of rats!" Callum piped up. "One of them had got out, and Fliss found it! And I want a rat of my own."

"Goodness me," Frankie's dad said. "Missing cats, found rats, mad kittens – whatever next?"

Just then the kitten came down from the curtain. He skipped across the floor, and began to lick the tiles where the milk had spilt.

"Can I give him some water with a little milk in it?" Frankie asked, and her mum nodded.

"Take him up into your room as soon as he's drunk it. And you'd better take his box with you – oh, and put some newspapers in

Muffin's old litter box. Is he house trained?"

"I don't know," Frankie said, and she went very slowly to fetch the milk.

CHAPTER FIVE

You should have seen us sitting in Frankie's bedroom! GLOOM. MEGA GLOOM. And then MEGA MEGA GLOOM.

That's not like us. If you know anything at all about the Sleepover Club you'll know we're usually falling about or cracking up about something. But there we were – and even with scrummy chocolate biscuits in front of us we all had faces as long as fiddles.

Frankie was sitting with the kitten on her lap. He was looking as if he'd never climbed a curtain in his life, and making this cute little purring noise.

Lyndz was staring out of the window. Rosie was slumped against the wall. Kenny was frowning at her feet. I was watching the kitten. I couldn't believe that Frankie couldn't keep him. I mean, my mum has *always* said no pets, but Frankie's got a dog, and a cat is much easier to keep. You don't have to take them for walks, and they don't need playing with the same way a dog does.

Thinking about cats made me remember Truffle, and I sat up.

"I'll have to take Callum home soon," I said. (I'd left him downstairs watching the Simpsons. He just LOVES the Simpsons.) "Are we going to make those notices about Truffle?"

No one answered at first, and then Lyndz suddenly leant forward. She pointed out of the window.

"Hey! Fliss – can you see a cat over there on the wall?"

I hurried to look, but I couldn't see any cat. Frankie got up and carried the kitten to the window so they could both look out.

"Oh – that's one of Mrs Brierley's cats," she

said. "She's got *dozens* of cats – I think she collects them or something."

"LYNDZ!!!" Kenny rushed to the window too. "If she collects cats maybe she's collected Truffle! Maybe she goes round the streets with a cat bag—"

Rosie nodded. "And she calls, 'Kitty, kitty'! And she has smelly fish heads in her bag—"

"And when they come running she snatches them up and hurries home to add them to her collection!" Lyndz said. Then she looked really worried. "Do you think she might have taken Truffle?"

"Only one way to find out," Frankie said. "We'll go and see!"

"We can't!" I said. "We can't march in and say, 'We've come to check out your cats'!"

"We could – we could offer to do odd jobs for her!" Frankie said. "My mum's always saying she's a poor old thing who could do with some help! We could say we're—"

"Boy scouts!" said Kenny. "My dad says boy scouts used to come round to his house once a year and say 'Bob a job!' And whatever you

43

asked them to do they did, and it only cost a bob. Dad says that's about five pence!"

"We *can't* be boy scouts," I said, and for some reason all the others cackled with laughter.

"It's good idea, though," Rosie said. "We could do – er—"

"Weeding!" Frankie said. "Her garden's full of weeds! And that would give us a brilliant excuse for spying on Mrs B and checking out the cats!"

Rosie moaned loudly. "I HATE weeding."

"Me too," said Kenny. "But detectives have to be ready to take on any disguise! Tomorrow we'll be the Sleepover spies – undercover in the garden!"

"I'd rather be a cabbage," Rosie said.

"You already are!" said Frankie, so Rosie threw a pillow at her. The kitten took off and Kenny dived for him and missed. Frankie threw the pillow back at Rosie, but Rosie ducked – and it landed FLOP!!! on the plate of chocolate biscuits.

*   *   *

When we had caught the kitten again and picked some of the biscuit crumbs off the carpet we went back to the plan.

"I'll ask Mum," Frankie said. "She's bound to say yes to us being helpful. Then we can knock on Mrs Brierley's door after school. She's always there in the afternoons."

Rosie nodded. "I expect she goes cat catching at night."

"Out in the dark, with the cats' eyes shining!" Kenny said.

"We won't wait until it's dark though, will we?" I asked.

"Who knows where the hunt will take us!" Frankie said, and she flung out her arms in an actorish way.

"We may have to go creeping through the bushes, and hunting in dark corners!" Kenny hissed.

"Hiding behind ancient creaking doors, while the slow, dragging footsteps pass by..." whispered Frankie.

"But it doesn't get dark until quite late," I said. "I can't stay out until then."

"Nor can we," Rosie said. "But we can imagine it—"

Lyndz sighed. "Wouldn't it be brilliant if Truffle really was there?"

"Tomorrow will reveal all!" said Frankie.

I got up again. "I'd better take Callum home."

"I'll come with you," Rosie said. "I promised I wouldn't be late."

"Me too," Kenny said.

"And me." Lyndz gave the kitten a little pat. "Goodbye, kitten."

"What are you going to do with him?" I asked.

Frankie groaned. "I don't know. Maybe Mum'll have a brain transfer in the middle of the night. I'll think about it tomorrow."

We all went quiet. Poor Frankie.

There was a small scuffling noise behind the door.

"Ssssh!" Rosie held up her hand, and we all froze. Rosie tiptoed to the door – and flung it open.

Who do you think was there?

Unfortunately it was Callum, and he was grinning.

"It's the pest!" Frankie and Kenny wailed together, and Callum grinned even more.

"How long have you been there?" Rosie asked him.

"Shan't tell you," he said. "Are we going home now?"

"YES!" I said, and I marched him down the stairs.

On the way home Callum asked me again about rats.

"Kenny says she keeps hers in the garage," he said. "Do you think Mum would let me do that?"

"NO," I said.

"Maybe Dad would let me have a rat at his house," said Callum. "Maybe I could keep a rat in his garage."

"Callum," I said, "Frankie and Kenny are right. You're a PEST."

"No I'm not," Callum said, but he didn't sound as cross as he usually does when I call him that. "Can we go to the pet shop again after school tomorrow?"

"No," I said. "I've got things to do."

"*Please*!" Callum said. "If you do, I won't tell Mum you're going to spy on the lady who catches cats!"

"*What*?" I said.

Callum giggled. "I heard *lots* of what you said! You're going to be a spy! You're going to be a spy!" And he hopped up and down, singing in a silly voice.

"Actually," I said. "You heard wrong. It was *you* we were talking about... it's *you* that's the spy!"

"NO I'M NOT!" Callum shouted. "I'll tell Mum you said that!"

I sniffed. "Tell her what you like," I said. "*I'll* tell her *you* were listening outside Frankie's bedroom door!"

Callum shut up then. We walked the rest of the way home without saying anything.

CHAPTER
SIX

When we met at school the next day Frankie was much more cheerful.

"I asked Mum about helping Mrs Brierley, and she said it was a mega-brilliant idea!" Frankie winked at Kenny. "She said it showed we were developing a sense of social responsibility, and she was really glad."

"Was she glad enough to let you keep the kitten?" Rosie asked.

Frankie frowned. "No. She said I had to take him back to the pet shop this afternoon."

"You can't," Kenny said. "It's half-day closing."

"Is it? Then I can keep him one more day!" Frankie brightened up at once. "He's getting ever so much tamer. He came down from the curtains almost as soon as I called him this morning!"

The horrible M&Ms went strolling past just then.

"Found your hot-water bottle yet?" they chorused, and then banged each other on the back with loud shrieks of laughter.

"They have to laugh at each other's jokes," Frankie said, very loudly. "No one else ever would."

"What's all that about a hot-water bottle?" It was Ryan Scott. I hadn't seen him coming, but he was suddenly right behind us. I started to smooth my hair down, but I stopped when I saw Frankie nudging Kenny. Frankie thinks I fancy Ryan Scott. Actually, I don't think there's anything wrong if I do. He's a very nice boy.

"Ryan – you don't want to know," Kenny said. "Those two are just *so* sad."

"They think it's funny to make jokes about my cat being lost," Lyndz told him. "She's been missing for three days now, and all they can do is make nerdish jokes."

Ryan looked really sympathetic. "My cat went missing once," he said.

"Did it come back?" I asked him.

"No," he said. "He'd been run over."

"Thanks a bunch," Lyndz said. "That makes me feel a whole lot better." And she went off across the playground. Frankie went with her, and so did Rosie and Kenny, but I didn't. I did think Ryan was trying to make Lyndz feel better, even if it didn't come out quite right.

"Tell you what," Ryan said, "tell Lyndsey she can come to my party. It's on Friday." I felt very strange right in the middle of my stomach. Ryan Scott was inviting *Lyndz* to his party! And not the rest of us! I think my mouth fell a bit open, because he gave me a funny look.

"I mean all of you," he said, as he spotted Danny McCloud. "Hey! Danny! Wait for me!" Then, as he dashed off to join Danny he shouted, "About seven o'clock! Bring any tapes you've got that are good!"

*   *   *

The others didn't think it was at all exciting that Ryan had asked us to his party.

"That's the night we're having a sleepover at my house," Lyndz said. "Don't you remember?"

"Couldn't we go the party and then have the sleepover afterwards?" I said. Frankie gave Kenny the sort of look that I know means they're sharing a joke and I'm not part of it.

"Who wants to go to Ryan Scott's party?" Kenny said. "It'll be full of boys with sweaty feet talking about football, football, football!"

"You like football," I said.

Frankie snorted. "We don't want to hear how Danny fell over in the mud seventeen times and Ryan would have scored if the goalie hadn't been in the way and how clever they all are."

"I wouldn't mind going," Rosie said. "We can talk about it afterwards! We don't need to stay for ages, but it might be fun for a little bit."

Lyndz said, "Why don't we vote?"

So we did, and Frankie and Kenny voted

against going. I was surprised when Lyndz
voted yes with me and Rosie.

"I like the idea of talking about it
afterwards," she explained. "And you never
know – there might be someone at the party
who's seen a missing cat!"

"We could make those notices about
Truffle," I said. "You know – what she looks
like, and your telephone number."

Lyndz gave me a huge smile. "Fliss," she
said, "you may be wet when it comes to Ryan
Scott, but you do have sensible ideas."

Even Frankie and Kenny thought it would
be a good idea to go to the party after that.

I was very pleased, but when I started to
talk about what we were going to wear they
said to wait until Friday.

"Today is operation *spy* day!" Frankie said,
and then the bell went and we had to go into
school.

I was lucky. Callum goes out to tea with his
weedy little friend Kevin on Wednesdays, so
he wasn't hanging around when we reached

Frankie's house. Of course we had to rush in to say hello to the kitten. He was in Frankie's room, all curled up in a little fluffy ball inside a shoe box.

We all oohed and aahed. He looked utterly cute, but we didn't wake him up.

"Work first," Frankie said sternly, but I bet if he had been awake she would have been the first to cuddle him.

We went downstairs and down the road. I had butterflies in my stomach, and I think Rosie did as well. Mrs Brierley's house was quite big, and it had a high wall all round it. There was a gate, but it did look quite creepy.

"See?" Frankie whispered. "Once they're caught the cats can never get out again!"

"Yes they can," I said. "Lyndz saw one on the wall the other night."

"That's only after they've been totally brainwashed never ever to escape," Kenny said.

Lyndz made a face. "You can't brainwash cats," she said. "They do just what they want!"

"Who's going to knock?" I asked. I didn't

want to hear any more of Frankie and Kenny's stories.

Frankie looked at Kenny, and Kenny looked at Frankie.

"We had an idea!" Kenny said, and she began to giggle. "We thought that we should find out if Mrs Brierley really *is* a catnapper!"

"How?" I asked.

"Well," Frankie said, "if she *is*, she'll want to catch as many cats as she can, won't she?"

"I suppose so," I said. Rosie nodded.

"What do you mean?" Lyndz asked.

Frankie leant against the wall of Mrs Brierley's house. "Well – if she hears two poor lonely cats yowling in the road outside, she'll think 'Aha! Two more pussy cats for my collection!' And she'll come rushing out to get them!"

"But we haven't got two lonely cats," I said.

Kenny and Frankie began to giggle again. "Yes we have," Frankie said, and she began to meow... and then Kenny joined in!

"WOWWWLLLLL... MERRRRROWLLLLLL... WOWWLLL!!!!" they howled. "WOWWLLL!!!!!"

Lyndz, Rosie and I began to laugh too. They looked so funny, and they kept rolling their eyes as they howled.

CRASH!!! The window went up above our heads.

Frankie and Kenny stopped dead, but it was too late.

SPLASHHHH!!!!!! A bucket of water sploshed right over them – they were *soaked*!!!! And a little old voice called out, "Go away! Go away, you horrid cats!" And then the window slammed shut again.

I don't think I've ever laughed so much. My sides hurt, and so did my tummy. I ached all over. We leant against the wall in a row, and Frankie and Kenny dripped as they laughed.

"I think it's time for Plan B," Frankie said at last. "Well – after Kenny and I have zoomed home and changed."

"That's right," Kenny said. "Mrs Brierley certainly doesn't rush out to catch cats!" And she began to crack up all over again.

"What's Plan B?" I asked.

"We knock on the door," Frankie said.

"Mum's already told her we're coming."

"You mean she's expecting us?" I asked.

"Oh yes," Frankie said. "But we did just want to check it out first."

"Oh," Rosie said, and if she was feeling like me she was thinking Frankie might have told us that before.

Frankie and Kenny flew home to change. Kenny had to borrow some of Frankie's clothes, and they're really different shapes, so Kenny looked really odd! Frankie's tall and thin, and Kenny's much smaller. Frankie's jumper nearly came down to her knees!

"OK!" Frankie said. "Time for Plan B!"

CHAPTER SEVEN

It was a scary moment when Mrs Brierley opened the door. I mean, what if our experiment was wrong, and she really and truly *was* a catnapper? What could we do? And how would we know which cats were napped and which were properly hers? It suddenly seemed very difficult.

"Do come in," Mrs Brierley said, and it was the same little old lady voice we'd heard coming out of the window. She *was* little, too – she wasn't any taller than Lyndz.

"I do hope you won't mind," she said, "but I've got some tea ready for you. Just to say thank you." She sighed. "It's *so* nice to see some company. All I see from day to day is my sister, or my dear cats!"

We trundled into the kitchen.

ACE!!!!!

The table was positively groaning under the scrummiest, most mega-delicious, FANTASTIC tea you have EVER seen!

We stood and stared, out eyes popping out.

Mrs Brierley smiled and looked really happy. She had such a nice face we all smiled back, and I felt as if I'd been mean even *thinking* nasty things about her. I was glad I hadn't told stories about her having smelly fish heads in her bag and catching cats at night – even if it had been a joke. And I was very glad indeed I hadn't been howling outside her house... although I had laughed a lot.

The tea was the best ever. There was one cake with chocolate icing and one with coffee icing. There were buns, and biscuits, and scones, and jam, and a huge bowl of clotted cream. We sat down, and I don't think I've EVER eaten so much. It was going to be really difficult to bend to do any weeding!

Mrs Brierley liked seeing us eat. She kept offering us more and more, and she liked talking too. She told us the names of all her cats, and I felt worse and worse because she turned out to be the sort of person who would never, not in a million zillion years, collect a cat that didn't belong to her.

We talked a lot too. We told her about the Sleepover Club, and she thought it was a BRILLIANT idea.

"I wish I'd had such lovely friends when I was young," she said. "There are so many more things that children can do nowadays. Parties, and sleepovers, and pretty clothes."

"We're going to a party on Friday," I told her. "Before we have a sleepover at Lyndz's house."

"*Are* you?" Mrs Brierley twinkled all over her face. "And what are you going to wear?"

I was just beginning to tell her about my new skirt with little silver stars on and the matching top with silver ribbons when Rosie kicked me under the table. Kenny frowned at me over the chocolate cake.

"We're all going," Kenny said, "but we're only going because we want to see if anyone has seen Lyndz's cat. Ryan Scott isn't our favourite person. He needs to get a life beyond football!"

"I don't suppose *you've* seen Truffle?" Lyndz asked hopefully. "She's a dark brown tabby and she's got three white paws."

Mrs Brierley jumped up from the table, and her eyes were full of tears.

"Oh!" She said. "You poor dear thing! There's *nothing* worse than losing a cat, and not knowing where it could be, or if someone's being unkind to it! *Of course* I'll look out for it!" And she hurried round the table and stroked Lyndz's shoulder – just as if she was a cat! Lyndz looked surprised, but I think she liked it.

"And do any of you others have cats?" Mrs Brierley asked when she'd sat down again.

Frankie took a deep breath – and she told Mrs Brierley all about the little black kitten, and how it was exactly like Muffin. Mrs Brierley listened, and her eyes were so bright she looked like a little bird.

"Well," she said, "I think there's a very easy answer if you'd like it. Why don't you bring your kitten here? He'll still belong to you, and you can come and see him as often as you want. I can promise you he'll be happy – he'll have lots of other cats for company, and there's a big garden for him to play in!"

"Oh! That would be *lovely*!" Frankie jumped up, and she hugged Mrs Brierley. It was Mrs Brierley's turn to look surprised, but she beamed at Frankie. Her spectacles were crooked from the hug, but she didn't notice. "Just don't forget to ask your mother," she said. "I don't want you doing anything your parents don't know about."

"Can I get him now?" Frankie asked. "I mean – I'll ask Mum first – but if she says yes?"

Mrs Brierley nodded, and Frankie flew out of the door.

You'd have thought that the kitten had lived in Mrs Brierley's house all his life. Frankie carried him in squealing and squirming like a furry eel, but the moment she put him on the carpet he sat down, looked round and began to clean himself. He even began to purr like a tiny engine.

"Well!" Mrs Brierley said. "I can quite see why you fell in love with that one! Have you given him a name yet?"

Frankie sat down beside the kitten. "I thought I'd call him Muffin," she said. "Like my last cat."

"That's a fine name," Mrs Brierley said. "And it looks as if he feels at home! Now, would you like to see the garden?"

I think we'd all forgotten that that was why we were there! Mrs Brierley was so kind and nice that she wouldn't let us do much weeding, but if there are five of you it's far more fun than when you have to do it on your own. She had to tell us which were the weeds – Rosie had a big battle with something that looked like a huge thistle, and then Mrs B said it was a special kind and she was quite happy for it to go on growing.

(I did wonder if Mrs B was quite relieved

when we stopped gardening. She said we'd done a great job, but she looked a little bit anxious about the thistle thing.)

We went back to Frankie's house for five minutes before we all had to go home. Frankie didn't want to leave Muffin, but Mrs B said she could come over as often as she wanted, and any of the rest of us could come too.

"It'll do the cats good to see some new faces," she said. She also said she'd be sure to look out for Truffle.

"I do see stray cats round here sometimes," she said. "In fact, there were a couple of horrible old tom cats fighting outside in the road earlier. I don't think they'll be howling outside my house again, though. I was very hardhearted and taught them a little lesson."

We couldn't say anything when Mrs B said that about the tom cats. Rosie made a gulping noise, and Kenny gave a sort of cough. Then we thanked her very very much indeed, and off we went.

On the way back we make a vow. We held hands and promised that we'd *always* look after Mrs Brierley.

"Do you think we should tell her that *we* are the tom cats?" Kenny asked.

Lyndz began to laugh. "I think she knew!"

"WHAT?" Rosie, Frankie, Kenny and I stared at her.

"Didn't you notice?" Lyndz said. "She never asked you two why your hair was wet. That was *weird*! I mean, how often do girls come to visit wearing odd clothes with drippy hair?"

"Oh." Kenny looked thoughtful. "And she did say she'd taught them a lesson—"

"She certainly did!" Rosie said. "You should have seen your faces when the water came down!" And we began to laugh all over again.

CHAPTER EIGHT

I had another good idea the next morning. Yes, I know that's boasting, but my mum always says that if you don't tell people when you're clever how can they ever know?

I was on my way to school and Callum was going ON and ON and ON about rats when I had my idea. Why didn't we ask Mrs Weaver if we could write and print out the notice about Truffle at school? The school computers are ace – you can do different borders and typefaces and rainbow colours.

I met Rosie and Kenny first, and they thought it was a dead smart idea, so we tried it out on Mrs Weaver when we saw her walking across the playground.

"Sounds like a good idea to me," she said. "Maybe we could get the whole class involved – a piece of descriptive writing that will wring the heart of anyone who reads it!" And she went into the staffroom.

Frankie and Lyndz arrived next, and they were keen too, although they weren't sure about the whole class having a go.

"We only need to use the ones we like," Kenny pointed out. "And we can run off lots of copies of those so we have plenty to take to Ryan's party."

"We don't want to be giving leaflets out *all* the time," I said.

Kenny tweaked my hair. "It's OK, Miss Flutter Heart. I'm sure there'll be loads of time for you to make eyes at Ryan and dazzle him with your starry skirt."

"How did you know I had a starry skirt?" I said.

"Don't you remember?" Frankie did a twirl under my nose. "You were giving Mrs B a stitch by stitch description for hours and hours yesterday."

"No I wasn't!" I said. "Kenny kicked me and I stopped!"

"I *didn't*!" Kenny said. "It was an accident!"

"OOOOOH!" It was the M&Ms. "Arguing, are we? And we thought you lot all cuddled up together with your hot water bottles!"

They staggered off holding each other up.

Rosie made a face. "Isn't it time you thought of a new joke?" she shouted after them.

"They're the saddest thing on earth," Frankie said in disgust.

"We're really going to have to do something about the M&Ms," Kenny agreed. "Anybody got any good ideas?"

But we hadn't.

When Mrs Weaver told everyone that we were all going to write a description of a cat and then think of a short piece of writing to go with it the only people who groaned were – guess!

YES!!! The M&Ms.

Mrs Weaver fixed them with a steely gaze. "Emma and Emily," she said, "I shall be particularly interested to see what you write. You are both clever girls, so I'm sure you will think of something suitable."

The M&Ms sat up and looked smug. "Can we work together, Miss?" they asked.

"That will be fine," Mrs Weaver said.

We all got into pairs or threes, but before we started to write Mrs Weaver asked Lyndz to stand up and describe Truffle. Then Mrs Weaver said were there any questions? Danny said something silly about did Truffle live in a chocolate box, but no one else asked anything. We all settled down to write.

After a while Mrs Weaver asked if any of us had finished, and would we like to read out what we'd written?

Lyndz went first. She read:

"Truffle is a special cat because I love her so much. She isn't very pretty, except I think she is. She is a dark brown tabby with three white paws, and is quite fluffy. When she left home she was wearing a green collar. The collar has my telephone number on it. If you have seen her PLEASE phone me – because I miss her."

Mrs Weaver said that was excellent, and then she went over to the M&Ms' table.

"Now, Emma and Emily," she said, "what have *you* done?"

They both smirked. It's the only word I can think of that exactly describes the look on their faces. Then Emma read out:

"Truffle is a pussy cat
Who warms my toes at night.
Her coat is brown and tabby
With three paws fluffy white.
Please tell me if you see her,
Skipping out there in the street,
And if you do please tell me,
Because she's very, very sweet."

Everybody clapped except us. Kenny and Lyndz looked at each other, and I saw Kenny cross her eyes. Frankie made being-sick noises, but very quietly, and Rosie rolled her eyes at me.

Of course Mrs Weaver thought the poem was stunningly clever and ace and the most excellent ever written.

"There, Lyndsey!" she said. "Wouldn't you like to use Emma and Emily's poem? I'm sure they wouldn't mind. I'll set the computer up for you at lunchtime… and I think you should thank them for their hard work."

Lyndz squirmed about in her seat, and then muttered, "Thanks a lot." The M&Ms sat and smirked and smirked.

Frankie stood up. "Please, Mrs Weaver, I think Lyndz should use her own piece of writing!"

Mrs Weaver didn't look that impressed. "Frankie," she said, "it was you and Lyndsey that suggested it should be a class project. I don't think you can change your minds now – especially when Emma and Emily have written such a lovely poem."

Frankie sat down.

*   *   *

The rest of the morning was one of the most gruesome we've ever lived through. The M&Ms never stopped grinning like a pair of horrible gargoyles, and they offered to write poems for everybody in the class. Even Mrs Weaver got fed up in the end, and told them to be quiet.

At lunchtime we stayed in and printed about twenty copies of the M&Ms' pathetic poem, and Mrs Weaver gave us a box to put them in to keep them clean. We left the box on the table by the computer; we didn't feel like taking it home.

"You don't have to use those," Rosie said as we trailed out.

"No," Frankie said. "We could type out your one on Dad's computer tonight."

Lyndz groaned. "Fancy having to *thank* the M&Ms. And I can't come round tonight. Mum says it's time I came straight home after school for once."

"Me too," Rosie said. "Are we still going to Ryan's party tomorrow? And then having a sleepover?"

"I'm not even sure about that," Lyndz said gloomily. "Mum was saying something about some old school friend of hers coming for the weekend. I'll tell you tomorrow."

The bell went, and we drooped back into afternoon school. It didn't feel as if anything was going to go right for us EVER again... but then things changed!

CHAPTER NINE

It was after school. We were chatting while I waited for Callum, when Rosie suddenly realised she'd left her bag behind. She dashed back into the classroom, and – *there were the M&Ms, secretly printing out loads of copies of their poem!!!*

As you can imagine, Rosie came zooming back to tell us.

"When they saw me," Rosie said breathlessly, "they switched the screen off double quick, but I could see the pile – even though Emma was trying to sit on it."

Our mouths fell open so wide they nearly

hit the concrete floor.

I just stared.

"Why ever would they do that?" Kenny asked.

"What did they say?" said Frankie.

"What did *you* say?" said Lyndz

Rosie grinned a wicked grin. "I remembered about being a detective," she said. "I waved, grabbed my bag and ran. I banged the door behind me as I went out… and then I crouched down outside and listened!"

"COOL!" said Frankie. "What did you hear?"

"I couldn't hear what they were saying," Rosie said. "But I heard the printer running again as soon as I was outside the door – so I *know* they think I didn't see anything."

"WOW!" Kenny's eyes were shining. "Those M&Ms are up to something again – but this time I think we might be one step ahead!"

"So what should we do?" I asked.

"One of us ought to sneak back in," Lyndz said. "See what they're doing now."

"I can't," Rosie said. "They'll be suspicious if it's me."

"HEY!" Kenny gave a huge jump in the air. "I've got it! Fliss, *you* can go! You can ask them if they've seen Callum!"

"ACE!!!" Frankie banged Kenny on the back. "They'll never suspect Fliss! They'll just think the pest has escaped again!"

I was halfway back to the classroom when I met the M&Ms coming towards me.

"Hi!" I said, "have you seen Callum?"

"Dear me," Emily said, "have you lost him? How careless! First it's a cat, then a brother! Mind you count your fingers and toes tonight!"

I didn't answer. I walked straight past.

Of course I knew Callum wouldn't be in the classroom – but I still went in. I thought I might do a little detecting too. The computer was switched off and everything was tidy – until I saw the wastepaper bin. It was stuffed full of crumpled up sheets of paper.

CLUES!!!! I thought, and I grabbed the top couple of sheets.

It was their poem, just as Rosie had thought. The two copies I had were a bit

76

blurry, so they must have thrown them out. I stood up, and glanced at it – and then I froze. I really did! You read about people freezing in stories, but I've never known what it meant before. But it's true – your arms and legs feel totally switched off. But my brain was working. I could still read. And this is what I read:

"Truffle is a pussy cat
Who warms my toes at night.
Her coat is brown and tabby
With three paws fluffy white.
Please tell me if you see her,
Skipping out there in the street,
And when you do please tell her,
I promise to wash my smelly feet!"

I wanted to zoom back to the others yelling at the top of my voice, but I didn't. I looked at all the other sheets of paper in the bin. The M&Ms had been working on the poem and changing bits, but – and isn't this a mega-brilliant bit of detective work? – I detected that the sheets on the top must have been the last dropped in the bin – so *that* must have been what they'd been printing out when Rosie saw them! I stuffed the two sheets of paper in my pockets and hared right out of school.

Kenny and Lyndz were sitting on the bench when I came bursting out. Rosie and Kenny were talking to Callum, who was looking very grumpy. What's new?

"I want to go HOME!!!" he said as soon as he saw me. "I want to go NOW!!!"

"Callum," I said, "if you are *very, very* good and give me *ten* minutes we'll go home past the pet shop."

That shut him up. He went skipping off to the water fountain.

The Sleepover Gang could tell from my face that I'd found something!!!! I reached into my pocket, and snatched out the pieces of paper with a flourish. Rosie grabbed one and Kenny grabbed the other, and Frankie and Lyndz peered over their shoulders.

"This is just that awful poem," Frankie said.

"What's so special about— OH!"

Lyndz and Kenny got to the same bit at the same time.

"RIGHT!!!" Kenny yelled. "This is WAR!!!"

They read it again. And again.

"Well done, Fliss," Lyndz said, and I glowed.

"What are we going to do now?" I asked.

Frankie was screwing up her face. "You know what I think? I think the M&Ms are going to swap the poems – so when we get to Ryan's party everybody reads *this* load of garbage!!!"

We stared at her. It seemed obvious now she had said it.

"Was our box of poems still there?" Frankie asked me.

"Yes," I said. "It was on the table."

"I know!" Kenny said. "Why don't we take our poems out of the box, and put something HORRIBLE in it instead – something that'll really make them shriek?"

"SPIDERS!" Rosie said. "We could fill it full of spiders!"

"YUCK!!!!!" I said. "I'm not catching spiders – not even to scare the M&Ms!"

"Nor me," Lyndz said.

"I can catch spiders," said a squeaky voice just behind us.

We jumped – it was Callum.

I was about to shriek at him for listening in to our conversation *again* when Kenny stopped me.

"Can you really catch spiders, Callum?" she asked.

"'Course I can," he said. "How many do you want? There's LOADS and LOADS in our shed."

"No there aren't!" I said.

Callum looked rather pink. "Yes, there *are*. I put them there."

Rosie clamped her hand over my mouth. "Well done, Callum!" she said. "Can you bring them to school tomorrow?"

Callum nodded. "Can I have them back after?"

"NO!!!!" I said.

"Callum," Kenny said, "if you bring the spiders in you can come to my house and play with my rat. Promise. Cross my heart and hope to die."

Callum thought about it. Then he looked at me. "And can we still go to the pet shop on the way home? You did say."

I gave in. "Yes," I said.

"FAB!!" Frankie began to dance around the playground. "Hey – Fliss – make sure you get here before the bell! And we'll have to watch those two *extra* carefully to make sure they don't swap the poems before we've done our dirty deed!!!!"

"Help!" Rosie looked at her watch. "I've got to go! Mum'll *kill* me!"

"Me too," Lyndz said.

"Can we go now?" Callum said.

"Yes," I said, and we did.

The next morning Callum and I walked to school one behind the other. Oh, I know the spiders were in a box inside another box, but I wasn't taking any chances.

The others were waiting.

"COOL!" Kenny said. "When will we put them in the box?"

"We'll have to do it at break time," Rosie said.

"I'll put the box on our table until then so they won't be able to fiddle with it."

"Do you know," Lyndz said slowly, "I think they'll try at the end of the day… in case we notice."

"That's settled, then," Frankie said. "Oh – and don't forget to bring your pyjamas tomorrow night. Mum says it's OK if we have a sleepover after the party."

"BRILLIANT!!!"

The morning dragged until break time. I kept looking at Kenny's bag. I knew the box of spiders was inside – what if they got out? But at least they had two boxes to eat their way through. YUCKKKK!!!!

Then – would you believe it? – when break time finally came it was raining, so it was wet play and nobody went out of the classroom at all. The only thing that cheered us up was that the M&Ms kept winking at each other, and sniggering. They had something planned – that was for sure. And they asked us about three times each if we were going to the party, and if we were going to give everyone one of their poems. Rosie had a secret peep to see if they'd already done a swap, but they hadn't.

It had stopped raining by lunchtime.

"Mrs Weaver, shall we tidy up the classroom?" Emily asked in her sweetest be-nice-to-the-teacher voice. "Emma doesn't feel very well, so we'd rather not go out."

We held our breath.

"No, Emily," Mrs Weaver said firmly. "You've been in all morning – a blast of fresh air will do you both good." And she swept us all out in a no-nonsense sort of way.

"Oh – Mrs Weaver!" Frankie popped up beside her. "Can I fetch my jumper from the coat pegs?"

"Hurry up, then," Mrs Weaver said, and Frankie scooted off, with a wink to us.

I don't think we've ever hurried back after lunch before – but this time we did. It was OK – we were there before the M&Ms. Mrs Weaver had stopped them in the corridor to ask

Emma how she was feeling – they looked *so* fed up!

I was even more nervous in the afternoon. The box was back on the table by the computer – but now I knew it was full of spiders! But first we had maths, and then we had history – and then – I can hardly tell you for laughing!

It was very nearly the end of school. We were all twitching. What if we'd been wrong? What if the M&Ms *weren't* planning to swap their poem for ours? And then Emily got up, and went over to the computer.

"Mrs Weaver," she said, "can I type out my project?"

Mrs Weaver was busy, so she just nodded. Emma got up next, and went over to the computer too... carrying her bag. She bent down, winked at Emily and pulled a pile of papers out of her bag – and then knocked our box on to the floor.

SCREAM!!!!!! The M&Ms were standing on the computer table clutching each other and shrieking their heads off. Paper was scattered all round them, while half a dozen fat spiders were heading for dark corners as fast as they could go.

OK, I admit it. I screamed too. *And* I leapt on to our table.

Mrs Weaver was *so* angry. She actually shouted at us all to be quiet … and *then* she picked up one of the pieces of paper. She only glanced at it at first, but then she frowned.

"What EXACTLY is going on here?" she asked.

And then it all came out. The M&Ms were so shaken that they told Mrs Weaver exactly what they'd done…

PHEW!!!!! We *almost* felt sorry for the M&Ms. But of course, there were the spiders to explain. So – we got a major earwigging too. We're all picking litter off the playground every break next week. But it was worth it!!!!

CHAPTER TEN

I bet you thought that was the end! But it isn't – because I haven't told you about the party.

No, it's OK. I know you may not want to know about what I wore – though it did look very nice. (No, I'm *not* boasting. Ryan said so. And so did Lyndz.) No – I wanted to tell you the most AMAZING thing.

We'd arranged to meet outside so we could all go in together. We always do that at parties. It means you don't have to stand around on your own. Anyway, Lyndz was the last to arrive. She looked puffed out.

"What's up?" Kenny said.

"Dad took me round to the cats' home," Lyndz said. "After all that fuss with the M&Ms I suddenly thought we *still* haven't done anything about finding poor Truffle. Dad was feeling sympathetic, so we went to look – but she wasn't there." Lyndz gave a huge sigh. "I think she's gone forever." And a tear rolled down her cheek.

Then Frankie did one of the nicest things ever. She swallowed hard, and she said, "Lyndz – if you like, you can have Muffin. He'll make you feel better – really, he will."

Lyndz shook her head. "Thanks, Frankie," she said. "But I don't want another cat. Not yet. I want Truffle. But thank you."

Frankie gave a sort of cough. "Let's go and get this over with," she said, and she rang Ryan's door bell.

Ryan's mum opened the door – and there, *right in the middle of the hall,* was Truffle!!!! She was was looking very thin, and her front paw was bandaged – but we all knew it was her. She knew Lyndz, too. She began to purr the loudest purr you ever heard – and Lyndz sat down on the doorstep and cuddled her and hugged her.

Ryan's mum was very nice. She told us she'd found Truffle crying in her back garden with her paw swollen right up. She'd taken her to the vet, and he'd treated the paw, but no one knew where Truffle came from. She wasn't wearing her collar – so it must have fallen off somewhere.

"Didn't Ryan tell you we'd taken in a lost cat?" she asked.

"No," Frankie said, and she looked very hard at Ryan when he came out to see what all the noise was.

Ryan went as pink as Callum does when he's done something wrong. "I didn't think it was your cat, honestly," he said. "You said yours had a green collar. And—" he shuffled his feet, "it was really nice having a cat again."

His mum gave him a funny look – half cross, half not. "But you can't have this one, Ryan," she said. "Not if it belongs to Lyndsey." She looked thoughtful for a minute while Ryan looked at the ground. "But how about we go to Mr Garez's pet shop tomorrow and see if he has any kittens for sale?"

Ryan looked so pleased I thought he was going to burst. "Really?" he said and when his mum nodded he squeezed her *so* hard. Then he saw us all looking and coughed and tried to look cool. But we knew he was thrilled really.

So – it was all happy endings. Lyndz had Truffle back, and when we had our sleepover that night Truffle sat on her toes *all* night, and Lyndz wouldn't move so we had to pass her biscuits and coke and stuff as if she was a queen or something.

And there are *more* happy endings! Muffin is EVER so happy at Mrs Brierley's house, and is growing huger and huger every day. We're always popping round to see him, *and* Mrs B of course.

What else? Oh – you remember Frankie's mum saying she couldn't have a kitten because of something that was going to happen next summer? Some kind of surprise? Did you guess what it was? I didn't.

FRANKIE'S MUM IS HAVING A BABY!!!!!

Frankie is so thrilled – you'd think no one had ever had a baby before. She's quite nice to Callum when he comes round to see Kenny's rat – I think she's practising on him.

One last thing. Don't laugh. Promise? Ryan asked me to go with him to collect his kitten.

This is Felicity Diana Sidebotham saying, "Thank you very much for your company."

See you!

Mega Sleepover Club ①

In *The Sleepover Club at Frankie's*, the gang decides to set up Brown Owl with Dishy Dave the school caretaker. But playing Cupid isn't as easy as they think... It's Lyndz's birthday in *The Sleepover Club at Lyndsey's*, and the gang plan a spooky video night. Only the spooks suddenly seem for real... And in *The Sleepover Club at Felicity's*, Fliss goes diet-crazy. But sleepovers and food go hand in hand, and the girls must find emergency supplies!

Three fantastic Sleepover Club stories in one!

Collins

www.fireandwater.com
Visit the book lover's website

Mega Sleepover Club ②

Fligg is desperate for a pet in *The Sleepover Club at Rosie's*, and volunteers to look after the school hamster for the weekend. Oh–oh... Kenny's horrible sister is out to make trouble in *The Sleepover Club at Kenny's* – have the Sleepover Club met their match? And in *Starring the Sleepover Club*, it's all fun and games with Fligg's mum's camcorder. Will the Sleepover Club discover screen stardom, or will their film be a flop?

Three fantastic Sleepover Club stories in one!

Mega Sleepover Club ③

The gang decides to form a pop group in *The Sleepover Girls go Spice*, except their secret rehearsal in the attic doesn't quite go to plan... *The 24-Hour Sleepover Club* sees the mates at loggerheads with their dreaded rivals, the M&Ms – and they soon find that revenge can be sickly sweet! And make way for chaos in *The Sleepover Club Sleeps Out*, when a school trip overnight to a local Egyptian museum provides a perfect excuse for terrifying the M&Ms...

Three fantastic Sleepover Club stories in one!

Order Form

To order direct from the publishers, just make a list of the titles you want and fill in the form below:

Name ....

Address ....

....

....

Send to: Dept 6, HarperCollins Publishers Ltd, Westerhill Road, Bishopbriggs, Glasgow G64 2QT.

Please enclose a cheque or postal order to the value of the cover price, plus:

UK & BFPO: Add £1.00 for the first book, and 25p per copy for each additional book ordered.

Overseas and Eire: Add £2.95 service charge. Books will be sent by surface mail but quotes for airmail despatch will be given on request.

A 24-hour telephone ordering service is available to holders of Visa, MasterCard, Amex or Switch cards on 0141- 772 2281.

An imprint of HarperCollins*Publishers*